The Resettling

My father and uncle were drinking beer in the kitchen. Uncle Tam's an easy-going man, jolly with a red face, and I've never seen him worked up except when Aunt Jessie set their flat on fire half-an-hour before he was due to go and see Scotland playing England at Hampden. It was missing the football rather than the fire that upset him, you understand.

I went into the kitchen to make some supper.

'Hello there lass,' said Uncle Tam. 'How're you doing then? Fine, eh?'

Only with reservations, I told him, since I was worried about my mother.

'Aye, your dad's said she's no been right. A good tonic'd set her up.'

'Tonic!' I began to slap butter on to bread. Men! They never want to face up to anything. 'Nothing short of getting her out of here'll sort her.'

JOAN LINGARD

Maggie
The Resettling

Pan Piper
PAN MACMILLAN
CHILDREN'S BOOKS

First published 1975 by Hamish Hamilton Children's Books

This Pan Piper edition published 1994 by Pan Macmillan Children's Books
a division of Pan Macmillan Publishers Limited
Cavaye Place London SW10 9PG
and Basingstoke

Associated companies throughout the world

ISBN 0 330 33290 2

3 5 7 9 8 6 4 2

A CIP catalogue record for this book is available from
the British Library

Phototypeset by Intype, London
Printed by Cox & Wyman Ltd, Reading, Berkshire

For Kersten, with love

CHAPTER ONE

I WAS in a thick, dark mood, of the kind you could cut with a knife. I have a variety of moods ranging from light and frothy to golden and peaceful, to black and leaden. This was definitely one for the lower depths.

I was standing in a street in Glasgow, one where I'd been born and had lived until a few weeks ago. Now monster machines were in the middle of tearing the place to bits, chomping, chewing, disgorging, tossing around chimney pots, doors, walls, floor. Homes. Yes, once they had been that, where fires had burned in the grates and folk had sat eating their tea and watching telly and laughing or crying. You could see the wallpaper they had laid on so carefully: blue with stripes, pink with flowers, green, yellow, red, torn to ribbons now, blowing in the wind. I remembered my dad papering our front room. Regency stripes, lilac and silver. Yuck! I had wanted something hot and jazzy at the time – I was in an orange phase – but he wouldn't listen. The regency stuff was good quality paper, he'd got it at a bargain price of course. Never mind the colour, as long as it was a bargain. 'Is it straight, Nan?' he'd kept asking my mother every two minutes from his perch on the ladder. And forever after she would

1

stare at the wall and say, 'That middle panel's no right, Andrew.' No longer! And now here was I longing to be back amongst the regency stripes and the old black kitchen range that I used to complain about being left over from the Ark.

I went so close that someone shouted to me to get back. I moved, just a little. Another side of the tenement building came tumbling down, and I got my school clothes covered with dust.

I turned away. Well, that was it! I went to collect my mother. She was having her hair set a couple of streets away, in one of those small hairdressing salons where they have two washbasins, three assistants, a pile of stodgy women's magazines full of babies' bootee patterns and two dusty-looking wigs in the window. They also had, propped behind the wigs, the picture of a hairstyle that might have been fashionable during the First World War, and then again, might not. My mother had been in there for more than two hours. They always take twice as many customers as they can cope with. If I was ever a client, which I never would be – nothing would persuade me to sit under one of those heat-belching hoods swathed in chiffon, unless it was a substantial financial inducement, that is – I'd complain like mad. But then I think the women quite enjoy it: a bit of chat, cup of tea, company. It's a social outing, next best thing to bingo.

I found my mother at the end of the row, hands folded over a dog-eared magazine on her lap, eyes shut, mouth slightly open. What I could see of her face and head looked kippered.

'She's just about done,' said the girl who was doing

her. Her name was Cathy and she used to live down the road from us.

'She looks it,' said I, and took a seat.

Cathy pushed up the drier from my mother's head, startling her. She jerked awake, not knowing for a moment where she was.

'Hi, Ma!'

'Maggie, what are you doing here?'

'Waiting for you. I told you I'd come for you.'

She shifted to the seat in front of the mirror where the combing-out takes place. Her face was the colour of a boiled beetroot. The things women suffer! For men, it's said. But my mother doesn't do it for my father. He hates her hair when it's just out of the hairdresser's. 'It looks like an overblown loaf,' he says. 'And all that muck you've got on it makes it look like steel wire.' Charming, isn't it? She does it to impress the neighbours: at least, that's what I tell her. And she tells me, 'Maggie McKinley, you're a right cheeky besom and no mistake! I only want to look nice.'

Cathy pulled out the rollers, dropping a few of the prongs on my mother's lap, and then she began to brush out the hair with long vigorous strokes. Watching her made me think of my friend Catriona Fraser whom I'd met when I was staying with my granny in Inverness-shire in the summer. Catriona was training to be a hairdresser. And thinking of Catriona led me naturally on to think of her brother James. I felt kind of crumbly inside when I started thinking about James and I didn't want to feel crumbly just then for I'd had enough at the demolition site.

'What have you been up to then?' asked my mother,

3

who is always inclined to think I have been up to something unsuitable. She eyed me in the mirror.

'I went to see the old place being pulled down.'

She turned sharply to confront me face to face and Cathy caught her in the eye with the hairbrush.

'Terribly sorry, Mrs McKinley.'

But she hadn't even felt the jab though her eye was inflamed.

'What did you have to go and do a thing like that for?' she demanded.

'I only believe in the evidence of my own eyes.'

She turned back towards the mirror with a 'Humph!' Her mouth was puckered into little lines. Cathy began on the backcombing, torturing the hair into weird tufts that stuck out all around my mother's head. It kills me seeing all that done to good healthy hair. I'm very solid on nature these days. I give five-minute talks on it at school. Purity. Natural development. Conservation. All that. I was converted during my summer in Inverness-shire. I wished it was summer again and I could be with James and Catriona and my granny. For a moment I thought I could smell pine trees – but it was only hair lacquer.

'So it's down then, is it?' said my mother.

'Yes. Flattened.' I spread my hands to demonstrate.

My mother took a cigarette from her handbag. She avoided my eye. I'm always telling her she should give up. Her hand shook as she lit it. She had lived in that flat from the day she got married until we were evicted.

'Don't know why they couldn't have let us alone. We were all right there, weren't we, Cathy?'

Cathy had been concentrating hard and was

gradually reducing the fuzzy bush to some kind of order. 'What's that, Mrs McKinley?'

'It's terrible getting put out your own home, isn't it?'

'I don't mind the new place,' said Cathy. 'At least it's modern.'

My sister, Jean, claimed she didn't mind it, either in spite of the smell of urine in the lift, and the grafitti. She said you got a good view of Glasgow. In my opinion they should pull the block down. They're starting to pull down some blocks like these.

Cathy seized the lacquer tin. She was a big girl with powerful hands and did everything with twice as much force as the other two assistants put together. Watching her made me feel like an eight-stone weakling, which I am. Cathy shot jets of lacquer over my mother's head as if she were attacking a nest of wasps with extermination gas. I retreated from the line of fire, not wishing to be contaminated by any of that gluey gunk.

Cathy held a mirror behind my mother's head.

'That's lovely, Cathy. Really nice.'

We could go. At last! Suffering doughnuts, it was about time! My mother blinked when we hit the daylight.

We took the bus home. We had to wait twenty minutes with the cold nipping our ankles until our number turned up. Before, we used to walk most places, but now that was not possible for we lived miles from the centre of the city. We inhabited the far-flung outskirts, a kind of no-man's-land between town and country. It was like being on the moon. And although

5

we had only been there for little over a month we knew it was not for us, except perhaps Jean, who could settle in Siberia if she had to. But the question was: what were we to do about it?

'We'll just have to put up with it,' said my father. 'I suppose we could apply for an exchange but one block of new flats'd be much the same as the next. What else can we do? We've no money to buy our own place.' Of course then he started on about what he should have done years ago – bought his own house, started his own business – which made me impatient. He's great at seeing what he should have done in the past but *not* what he should do in the present.

'There must be something we can do.'

'What, madam?'

I would think about it, I promised him, and had done endlessly, even in school when I should have been concentrating on the Napoleonic wars or the novels of D. H. Lawrence, but so far had had few sane ideas. Lack of money is undoubtedly a drawback. My English teacher says I resort too often to truisms.

'I'll be glad to get my shoes off,' said my mother as we got off the bus at the terminus. She clung to my arm.

'You're looking better.'

'It's done me good to get out.' She glanced upwards at the high, looming block and shuddered. She hated being in there, said it was like Colditz, but she hated going out too. It was the lifts: they gave her the willies. She would walk down rather than use them, but it was a long hike up eleven flights. Sometimes we had to walk, when the lifts were out of order. That was not unknown. My mother had dreams in which the lift was plummeting downwards, taking her with it, trapped and screaming. Once or twice she had wakened screaming. Her nerves had started to play up really badly, and now she was living on tablets night and day. She was lonely too, missed neighbours and family dropping in. People didn't pop in and out of these high flats. It was a common enough problem in modern society, I told her, which annoyed her. I'm good at passing on snippets of information to my family that irritate them, when I only intend to offer comfort and show that they are not alone in their afflictions.

Outside the block we saw my friend Isobel talking to a boy. At least she used to be my friend, we'd known one another since we could stagger, but recently we'd grown apart. The trouble was that she had left school at the end of the summer term and was working; she went out nearly every night and thought I was a swot because I had to stay in and study and she had lots more money to spend than I. Our life styles had diverged: that is the best way I can put it. I felt sad about it but didn't see what I could do. We still spent an evening together sometimes and enjoyed ourselves.

'Hi, Isobel!' I called.

'Hi, Maggie!' she called back.

There were some small boys fighting in the vestibule. We skirted them and got into the smelly grey lift. My mother held tight to my arm as the doors slid shut. I don't like lifts either but I let my natural laziness triumph over my aversion in this case. Someone had scrawled the letters of a gang over the walls. My mother shook her head at it although youths had written over

7

the walls of our old tenement too. But no flaws here escaped comment.

We sailed swiftly upwards, without mishap. My mother breathed with relief when the lift doors slid open and released us.

My sister Jean and brother Sandy were already home. We heard Jean's record player and Sandy's transistor as soon as we opened the front door. My mother went straight into the sitting room, kicking off her shoes as she went, and switched on the television.

'I'll make you a cup of tea,' I said.

Through the open doorway of our bedroom I saw Jean lying on her bed reading a magazine. She glanced up.

'There's a letter for you.' She nodded at the dressing table. 'Looks like Lover Boy's writing.'

I pounced on it. It was a long fat white envelope, franked with an Edinburgh postmark. I took it to the kitchen clutched to my bosom and closed the door behind me. For a moment I just stood there studying my name and address written in his strong, neat handwriting. Silly old fool that you are, McKinley, you'd think you were a female in one of those stories Jean soaks up!

Before I opened it I put on the kettle. Sometimes, faced with a treat, I am impatient and cannot wait; at other times I delay, savouring the moment when it will be mine. I slit open the envelope carefully and took out the folded pages. There were six of them, close written on both sides, and on the last page, at the bottom were the words: 'Much love, James', followed by ten kisses.

I sat by the window to read it, and as I read I forgot that I was sitting in an eleventh-floor flat. I was back in my granny's glen walking with James along the twisty uneven road smelling the pine trees and all the other glorious scents of the undergrowth; and the burn snaked along on our left, disappearing now under the humped-back bridge where the cows liked to drink at morning and evening, and above us were the hills green and brown and purple. . . . My longing for the glen was so strong that it felt like an ache at the back of my throat. I shook myself, looked out and saw another block of flats rising up from the ground, and, to my right, another. I was suffering from homesickness! It was funny really, for I used to hate the glen and felt so lonely in it that I had wanted to shrivel up and die.

James wanted to know when I was coming to spend a week-end in Edinburgh. We had not met since the end of summer, and it was now October. In every letter he had asked when I would come, and I had always written back, stalling, saying yes, I would come, I wanted to, but I had a job on Saturdays and needed the money, my mother was ill, or we were in the middle of moving. All of the reasons were true but they were excuses also, for although I did want to see him part of me felt unsure about seeing him in his own home in Edinburgh. I had only known him in Inverness-shire, in that remote and beautiful glen. Perhaps I wanted him to remain a part of that. Perhaps I was afraid he might be different in Edinburgh. Or perhaps I was afraid that the magic might be gone. The truth was that I was somewhat muddled. Situation normal! But now, reading his letter, I wanted to see him a lot, and knew I would have to go to Edinburgh soon. If not, he said, he would come to Glasgow.

'What in the name's going on here, Maggie McKinley?' spluttered my mother.

She had reason to splutter for the kitchen was full of steam. I dived for the kettle switch, spluttering too as the gushing white vapour filled my throat. Then I flung open the window.

'You've aye got your nose stuck in something.' My mother sighed and shook her head. Frequently it was a book in which my nose was stuck, as she put it, for I often read whilst I was making toast or boiling milk. Needless to say, we have a lot of burnt toast and boiled-over milk in our house. But it's so boring just to stand staring at things, for when you do it's the old case of the watched kettle never boiling; it's only when you take your eyes off that you get any action.

'I've got a letter from James.'

'James?'

'James Fraser.'

'Oh, that laddie you met at your granny's place.' She took up the kettle and insisted on making the tea herself. I was useless and had best stay out of her road.

'Do you mind if I go to Edinburgh for the weekend? James wants me to come and stay with his parents.'

She shrugged. 'It's up to you. But what about your job?'

'I can give it a miss for one Saturday.' I worked in a department store in the city centre.

'I'm glad you've plenty money. It's more than I have.'

Giving up the money didn't please her, but it was only I who would suffer, as I pointed out, for with the money I earned I bought all my own clothes, books, records, etc. The only thing I took from my parents was food. Plus heat, light, toilet rolls, etc., as they pointed out. That was more than enough to take at my age, in their eyes. They had both started work at fifteen, and now here was I at sixteen still at school and proposing to spend two more years there and then four at university. I wanted to read for an honours degree in anthropology, having been inspired by Margaret Mead and Laurens van der Post at an early age. At thirteen I had been desperate to take off for the Kalahari and see the bushmen for myself, or to New Guinea to look for head-hunters. Whenever my mother contemplates me not earning my own living until I am twenty-two years old, so that I can learn about the customs of primitive peoples who inhabit places very far-flung from Glasgow, she is beside herself with amazement. She is proud of me, in her own way, which means that she grumbles about me at home and brags about me to the neighbours.

'I'm baby-sitting tonight,' I said. 'For my English teacher.'

Then she grumbled about me coming home across the town late at night and I said that he would bring me back safely in his car so she didn't have to add that to her list of worries. I was also baby-sitting for someone the following evening too, so I was making a bit of extra money this week.

She put the frying pan on to heat and began to cook haddock for our tea. I went back to the window

11

to look out. Grey dusk was gathering between the tall buildings and a few of the windows were already lit. One of the good things about being high up was that you could see for miles on a clear day, round the edges of the other skyscrapers, that is. My mother didn't like seeing for miles: it made her uneasy. The flats across the street had been enough for her at the old place; she could see who was cleaning their windows and lay forth about the folk who never took their curtains down to wash from one year's end to another. She could also hang out of our own window and watch what was going on in the street below. If you'd hung out of the window here you'd have felt you might get vertigo, and there was nothing much to see anyway, except some grey asphalt, a bit of patchy grass and some sickly trees that hadn't quite taken.

I peered down and after a moment saw my father's old car come chugging into the car park. I couldn't hear it coughing from up here but I knew it would be.

'Here's Dad.'

'You'd better get the table set for me then.'

'I will. In a minute.'

I watched him getting out of the car with his bag of tools. He's a plumber.

'Come on, girl, now!'

I moved. The table was set before my father opened the door. He hates to come home from work and find the table bare, and hates even more to come home and find the house empty.

Over tea I told him that I had witnessed the demolition of our old home. He grunted and went on eating. Then I told him I was going to visit James Fraser at the week-end. He grunted about that, too. He was not too keen on James, not that it was James's fault, but he and his father had saved my granny's life when her house went on fire and my father found it difficult to be under such a large obligation to them. I could seldom get him to discuss the matter.

'Going to have a posh week-end, are you?' said Jean and giggled.

Really, sisters can be so sick-making! I gave her one of my withering looks, which never have any effect on anybody, and got up to clear the table. My family, of course, does not understand me, except perhaps for my granny, who understands me better than I care for at times.

'The Frasers are really nice people,' I said loftily, scraping the remains of Jean's fish into the bucket. 'They are not at all posh.'

'Sound right toffee-nosed from what we've heard,' said Sandy.

He and Jean then began to make stupid remarks about toffee-nosed people from Edinburgh, which kept them amused until they had finished eating. They are easily amused. I left them to it and departed for the house of my English teacher.

The Scotts' house was in a state of chaos, which was nothing unusual and didn't bother me a bit. Mr Scott's wife, Janet, was a graduate in German and very keen on doing translations; she was better at that than looking after a house and two small children, though this she did at the same time and they were all quite happy. I called her Janet – she had asked me to – and we got on great together. I got on great with Mr Scott

13

too – he had never asked me to call him Colin and I was glad for I would have found it embarrassing – so I enjoyed going to their house. I thought that if James came to Glasgow I would bring him to visit them.

'How's your mum?' asked Janet.

I shrugged. 'Much the same. I think my dad's real worried about her, he never says much but I'm sure he is underneath.'

'You'll have to get him to apply for a transfer,' said Mr Scott.

'Getting him to move is like trying to shift Ben Nevis. He's all for letting things be.'

The Scotts went off to the cinema, I put the children firmly to bed, threatening them with all kinds of things which made them laugh, and retreated downstairs to an armchair by the fire in the sitting room, where I settled myself comfortably with my writing pad on my knee. It was nice not to have a television, transistor and record player all going in the background.

First I wrote to my granny, giving her all the family news which she would not be much interested in, since she had seen little of Jean or Sandy, or even my mother, who only leaves Glasgow for places like Blackpool or Morecambe and I told her also that I was going to visit the Frasers. She would be pleased about that; she liked James very much. 'Maggie's going to visit young Jamie Fraser,' she would tell her neighbours, and they would all nod knowingly.

Then I wrote to James.

CHAPTER TWO

JAMES WAS to meet me at Waverley Station. I could imagine him standing on the platform, blue eyes serious, brows drawn slightly together under the overhanging lock of fair hair, as he watched for the arrival of my train. My heart began to thump as we emerged from the dark tunnel into the light of Princes Street Gardens. I got up to put on my jacket and lifted my stuff from the rack. I had everything in two plastic carriers. I am notorious for my carrier bags, and as I was leaving my mother gave me a tirade about going to visit folk — especially posh folk like the Frasers — looking like a travelling gypsy. They would think we didn't have such a thing as a suitcase in the house! And I should have dressed myself up a bit more too, instead of wearing those old jeans with that old shirt and about sixty-five thousand strings of wooden beads round my neck. I had in fact dressed myself up to begin with, put on a dress and made up my face, but then had taken it all off for James had never seen me in anything but jeans and he might just stand and laugh at this new apparition of me. But now I was thinking maybe I should have dressed up more after all, for James himself might turn up in a good suit or even school uniform, since it was Friday afternoon. The idea of that made me giggle.

I looked up at the castle towering high on our right and glanced across at Princes Street on the other side. I didn't know Edinburgh very well, for most of my visits there had taken place on Glasgow public holidays when half the populace of Glasgow empties into Edinburgh to visit the same kind of shops they could go to any other day of the week at home. But it makes a change, as my mother used to say.

As soon as the train stopped I had the door open and was out. Waverley is an open station so I was able to walk straight out. James was waiting, just as I'd expected. I dropped my carrier bags and went forward to meet him. He swooped me up in his arms and birled me right round, the way kids do. I was gasping and laughing, and then he kissed me, which felt just right. We were standing in the way of everyone, which was not endearing us to those in a hurry.

'Maybe we should move ourselves,' said James.

He rescued my bags; we took one each, and held hands with the free ones. Now that I had time to notice I saw that he, too, was wearing his old jeans from the glen days. I laughed out loud, I felt so happy.

'It's great to see you, Maggie!'

'It's great to see you, James.'

We grinned at one another like a couple of loons all the way up the slope out of the station on to the street. James said that he could have brought his father's car but had not since it was not far to walk to his house and he didn't want us to get there too quickly.

'As soon as we get in Catriona will pounce on you. And Mother. And Father. And probably Grandfather, too.'

I had not realised that his grandfather lived with them. But then there was a lot I did not know about James. It had not seemed necessary to know it in the summer; now I must. It appeared that their house belonged to his grandfather, and he occupied one floor. He had been a solicitor, and was, as I was about to find out, very well-off, by my standards, anyway. He had been disappointed when his son did not follow him into the law and had thought teaching a bit of a come-down. Amazing, isn't it?

'Though he's come round now,' said James.

I laughed. 'That's good.' I supposed he had not yet come round to the idea of his grand-daughter being a hairdresser.

We crossed Princes Street, which I scarcely saw since I was too busy looking at James, went up the hill and then down into the New Town. This was the Georgian New Town, James explained to me, and it was here that they lived.

They lived in Heriot Row, the street where Robert Louis Stevenson grew up. It has houses only on one side, which form an elegant terrace, and facing them are private gardens. It was a bit formal for me but I could see it was elegant and really rather splendid. I felt myself go quiet inside.

'Come on,' said James. 'This is it.'

We went up a flight of steps into a hallway which I suppose you would describe as gracious, where the ceilings seemed to soar for miles above us and were decorated with elaborate cornices that looked like the icing they put on wedding cakes. Not cosy exactly. But then I've been brought up on a different scale, you could say!

'We live on the ground floor and basement mostly,' said James. 'Grandfather has the first floor, we sleep on the second floor, and then the rooms in the attic we use as workshops and general messing around rooms. Let's go down to the kitchen.'

He guided me down the stairs to the basement and as soon as we opened the kitchen door everything was all right. The Frasers had not changed. Mrs was making an apple pie and had flour all over her face and arms, Mr was wearing an old jersey with a hole in one arm and was trying to mend something that Mrs clearly felt he should be able to mend but couldn't, and Catriona was reading an article in a magazine on how to make yourself more alluring. They all dropped what they were doing to greet me, and soon we were chatting ninety to the dozen and drinking tea and sampling Mrs Fraser's hot scones just out of the oven spread with thick strawberry jam that she had made in the summer at the glen. The kitchen was piled high with news-papers, magazines, books, Mr Fraser's do-it-yourself tools and clumps of seaweed. The latter smelt quite a bit and James later removed it to the outside scullery. It was for a project on pond life for his mother's class of Infants. Also in the scullery were rocks, shells, sand, mud and some strange-looking creatures in a jar of water. My mother would do her nut if she had to have all that clobber in the house.

'We virtually live in the kitchen, Maggie,' said Mrs Fraser, telling me what I could see with my own eyes. 'You don't mind our mess, do you?'

'I love it,' I said happily, and wondered why on earth I'd been so stupid to wait so long to visit them.

'Come on and I'll show you your room, Maggie,' said Catriona, who was obviously dying to get me on my own so that we could indulge in some girls-only chat. I was not averse to the idea myself, so I accompanied her up the stairs to the room which I would share with her for the week-end. We sat on her bed.

'You've cut your hair,' I said. She'd had long thick blonde hair which I had envied, and now it was short and frizzed. Almost like mine, except that mine does it naturally and won't do anything else.

'Do you like it?'

'I preferred it long.'

She pouted. 'I wanted a change.'

I could understand that. Once I tried to grow my hair and iron it straight, and in true McKinley style had only managed to singe it so badly that I had had to have it cropped really short, and even then everyone had twitched their noses for days afterwards when I passed. I asked about her work, which she said was okay, but was a bit boring whilst she was at the stage of doing all the shampooing and cleaning-up jobs. I didn't know how she put up with all that, but I suppose if you want the end result enough you'll put up with anything. She talked a bit about the other girls, but I could sense there was something else on her mind, something that was getting ready to bubble up and spill out.

'Don't tell me you've fallen in love, Catriona!'

She had. She blushed a nice pink right up to her frizzy curls. He was a hairdresser, too, though he was fully qualified and was an absolutely fantastic stylist, and his name was Alexander. Yes, and believe it or not he used the whole handle, did not shorten it to Alex or Sandy.

'It sounds better for a hairdresser,' said Catriona. 'Alexander takes his work very seriously. He's thinking of setting up on his own soon, though it's still a secret and – ' she lowered her voice, ' – he's going to take me along with him. Mother won't want me to change jobs. She doesn't like Alexander.'

'She's met him, then?'

'I brought him home once.' Catriona sighed. 'It was a disaster.'

'But you know your mother – she takes a wee while to get used to things.' She had taken a while to get used to me, but had in the end, more or less.

James came to tell us that dinner was ready. We ate in the dining room, for Grandfather joined them for the evening meal and he adamantly refused to eat dinner amidst the clutter of the kitchen. Breakfast was different. He was all for the Civilised Life, you could see that by the way he took his napkin from its silver ring, unrolled it neatly and spread it across his knee, and the polite way in which he offered me everything first.

He had smooth silver hair and a sort of silver voice too, very clear and exact. He was the kind of old guy whom you felt must have been born with a whole rackful of silver teaspoons in his mouth. His back was very straight and he wore a dark expensive suit with a dazzlingly clean white shirt that was unlikely to have been washed by Mrs Fraser. For all her hectic activity she never actually produces things of that order. Maybe he threw his shirts away after each wearing! He was certainly a far cry from my granny in her wrap-around floral overall, ancient grey skirt and men's boots.

The funny thing was that when I looked at Grandpa Fraser I could see James in him. James had that same straight back, the same way of holding his neck, of smiling, even. James was particular, too, about his clothes, even when he wore jeans, for he was always neat and meticulous and would never wear sweaters with holes in them the way his father did. I had a feeling that at seventy James would be more like his grandfather than his father. I find all that kind of stuff dead interesting. Hm, yes. . . . And at eighty-three will I wear men's lace-up boots and a wrap-around overall?

The dining room was a bit overawing. It had been decorated and furnished by his grandparents, James told me later. We ate at a dark oak table with carved legs ending in lion's paws, sat on painfully hard high-backed oak chairs, ate with heavy silver cutlery that clattered if you were clumsy enough to drop any (and of course I was) and our plates were ancient and gold-encrusted. The sideboard was fantastic, dark oak again, solid, enormous in width and height, topped with a large mirror, and it was carved with lions' heads and claws and all sorts of other objects which I could not identify in the light flickering from the candles in the silver candelabra. Wild stuff all that!

But the food was good. One thing I will say for Mrs Fraser is that she's a great cook. Another funny thought that crossed my mind sitting there was that she didn't really belong amongst all these antiques. In fact, the only ones who did were James and his grandfather.

His grandfather questioned me about my school,

my family and my ambitions for the future. He was very lawyer-like but terribly nice with it and seemed to be really interested in the problems of my family's housing, and thus encouraged, I launched into full details. The Frasers enjoy having other people's problems to chew over – this I had discovered when my granny had a few – but they also try to find solutions and part of my reason for telling them was in the hope that they might be able to think of something.

'If we don't do something I think my mother'll have a nervous breakdown,' I said. And for the first time I realised it was quite possible. I felt sick.

'I don't suppose your father has any capital?' said Grandfather Fraser.

'I think he's got a few hundred put by – he's very cagey about money – but nothing more.'

'Why doesn't he start up his own business?' suggested Mrs Fraser. 'He wouldn't need much capital and plumbers are always in demand.'

'It's a good idea to start up one's own business,' said Catriona, jumping in. 'Don't you think so, Mother? I'd like to.'

'Yes, dear, sometime. When you're qualified and have some experience.'

'I don't see why I should wait for that. I mean, if I could go into business with someone who was qualified.'

But they were not listening to Catriona, or taking her seriously, for they did not know what I knew. They were thinking about my father and the possibility of him setting up in the plumbing business. Andrew McKinley, business man! The image didn't seem to fit somehow but Mrs Fraser, who had met him on one occasion, did not seem to find anything odd in the idea, and Mr Fraser senior said that he wouldn't need a huge amount of money to get going. We entered into a technical discussion which bored Catriona, who every now and then said that *she* would like to start a shop of her own.

'The thing to do is to find a shop to rent,' said Grandfather Fraser. 'One at not too high a rent, of course.'

They were waxing enthusiastic now, getting quite carried away by the idea.

'You never know,' said Mrs Fraser, 'you might find one with living premises at the back. Or overhead. Pity I'm not in Glasgow to help you look.'

She was right about that, for with Mrs Fraser heading the search no suitable shop would escape detection. By the time we rose from the table it was settled: my father was to go into business with my uncle (my mother's brother who is also a plumber) and I was to find them suitable premises with living quarters if possible. It would take my mother's mind off her problems, said Mrs Fraser: take her out of herself, which was what she needed. The only thing remained was for me to inform my father. Only!

'I'll come through to Glasgow and help you look,' promised James.

After we'd helped with the dishes we went out for a walk through the dark streets. It was a crisp, clear evening with a bite of frost in the air but I felt as warm as pie with James's arm round my waist. The trees looked pretty in the street lights; we could see their colours – red, gold, orange, brown – glistening; and

23

underfoot our feet scuffled through the fallen leaves.

On Saturday morning he insisted on taking me up Arthur's Seat, which is a kind of mountain shaped like a lion, or a seat for Arthur, whatever way you look at it, in the middle of the city. '*Hill*, Maggie!' said James. 'It's only a thousand feet or so.' Those Frasers! A thousand feet to them is like a gentle incline suitable for an eighty-year-old to take a stroll on. Anyway, I let him haul me up over the wet grass and I actually quite enjoyed myself, especially the bit where you come up to the top and then you stand and survey the whole scene below. Fantastic! There was the whole city spread beneath us, rooftops, towers, spires, streets and parks, and behind it the blue Firth of Forth with the Fife coast beyond. And the sun shone from a clear blue sky with little smudges of white cloud trailing across it. Remember that day in the glen, we said, when we climbed the hill? Remember? There was nothing we had forgotten.

'We're going up the glen for New Year,' said James. 'You must come with us.'

'I'd love to!' I jumped at the idea, then I thought of my mother who would not like me to be away from home at such a time. Our family always gathers to see the old year out.

'Couldn't you miss it just this once? You'd like to spend it with your granny too, wouldn't you?'

I would, of course, and there might not be many more chances to do it, since she was eighty-three. I promised James I would think about it, sound out the idea with my mother. I would have a lot of things to sound out with my family when I got back to Glasgow.

They'd be saying, 'Maggie McKinley, maybe you'd better not go there again if you're going to come back with all these daft notions in your head!' The trouble with my family is that anything new is daft until they've got so well used to the idea that it is then old. The Frasers are the complete opposite, contemplating buying a croft in Wester Ross one moment and a farmhouse in the Dordogne the next, though James says it's nearly all talk. They enjoy the talk, though, and the anticipation, and you never know but one of these days they might be off growing artichokes in Southwest France and trampling their own grapes underfoot. I like this side of them. Catriona's the only one of them who would not thank you for a farmhouse in France. All she wanted then was a hairdressing salon in conjunction with Alexander. Well, we all have our ambitions, and one person's is no crazier than the next, I suppose. But when I met Alexander I thought Catriona's was pretty crazy.

Catriona was dead keen that I should meet him so she arranged it for Saturday afternoon. James and I were to meet them at an appointed time in a coffee bar. We were half-an-hour late – we had been dawdling around and lost track of the time – so we didn't start off on the best footing. We could see that Alexander looked annoyed, and Catriona anxious, and they did not appear to be talking to one another. I apologised profusely, saying that it was all my fault, I had dragged James round the shops and you know what I'm like when I get going! I ran myself down until I was out of breath and dying for a cup of coffee. Alexander, once the annoyance was banished from his pretty face, smiled all the time. He had a plastic smile that you felt you could peel off if you'd the nerve to try. I hate people who smile all the time: it gets so boring to see them twinkling away, flashing their white teeth and expecting you to smile back. I smiled very little at Alexander. He was too pretty for me and his hair too carefully arranged. James told me later that I was incredibly prejudiced and had far too many preconceived notions about what people should or should not be. But who hasn't? I asked him. He said I'd have to start working on mine before I would make much headway as an anthropologist. 'An open mind, Maggie, that's what you need!' he said. I stuck my tongue out at him. Very infantile!

When I asked James if he liked Alexander he wouldn't commit himself. He shrugged and said that Alexander was no concern of his, so I told him that he should be, since he was involved with his sister. James said he had no intention of being concerned about all Catriona's boyfriends, so then I suggested that Alexander might be after Catriona's money, which made James roar with laughter.

'What money?'

'He might think she's rich,' I retorted, and James said I was funny. Ha, ha! I walked off, he caught up with me and we had a slight spat which only lasted two minutes.

Our meeting in the coffee bar could hardly be called a howling success. James said very little, Catriona prattled nervously, and I drank two cups of coffee and ate three doughnuts.

'Are you hungry?' asked Alexander.

'Yes.'

'You'd think we didn't feed you properly,' said Catriona.

'Oh, you do! It's just all this fresh air I've been getting – I'm not used to it. I'm out of training since I've been back in Glasgow.'

Catriona and Alexander left shortly to go to the cinema. Catriona asked if we would like to join them but both James and I said simultaneously, 'No, thanks very much.' We didn't have enough time together to waste any going to the cinema.

Catriona did not come home until after eleven. Mrs Fraser was as jumpy as a grasshopper all evening, never sitting down, going out to the pavement to look along the street and sending James and me along to the corner three times to see if Catriona was coming.

'Stop fussing, Elizabeth,' said Mr Fraser, who was trying to read. You'd think he'd have known her well enough by that time to know that she was not going to stop fussing, because she couldn't. Any more than she could sit still without doing something.

'But she's missed her dinner. She hasn't had anything to eat since lunchtime.'

'She had a jam doughnut when we saw her,' I said.

When Catriona came in she refused to answer the stream of questions her mother fired at her. Mrs Fraser lectured her on the dangers of being abroad on the streets of Edinburgh at this hour of night, making the place sound like Chicago in the Twenties. Of course it was not the dangers of the streets that were worrying her. Catriona went off to bed.

At midnight Mrs Fraser yawned and said brightly that she thought it was time we all retired, whilst fixing

James and me firmly with her eye. She was certainly not going to allow us to sit up after they had gone to bed.

'I thought we might all go out for a walk on the Pentlands before lunch, tomorrow,' she said. 'They're the chain of hills you can see to the south of the city, Maggie.'

'I am going to take Maggie to the Botanic Gardens tomorrow,' said James.

'I've got history essays to correct for Monday,' said Mr Fraser.

I went up to join Catriona, who was awaiting me to demand, 'Well, what did you think of Alexander?'

'I thought he was fine.' I knew I was unconvincing, but I am a bad liar.

'You didn't like him, did you?'

'Look, Catriona, I only saw him for twenty minutes – '

'And all that time you ate doughnuts! You were horrible, you didn't even try to be nice to him, you just sat and ate doughnuts!'

I thought she was going to burst into tears. I struck my chest a blow, hurting myself, which was not intended, and declared, 'I admit to the cardinal sin of gluttony! Do what you will with me! Punish me. . . .'

'Oh Maggie,' said Catriona, and giggled.

We talked till three in the morning.

Mrs Fraser had to call us about ten times for breakfast before we responded. As we sat eating hard bacon and eggs she told us that we were silly girls giving up our beauty sleep and we had bags under our eyes.

James told me that he thought I was beautiful, bags

or no bags, as we walked under the trees in the Botanic Gardens. I still felt a bit embarrassed when he said things like that to me. Part of me wanted to giggle, but I couldn't, for he looked so earnest.

The trees were dropping leaves all over us as we passed beneath. They were so incredibly and sizzlingly beautiful and the gardens so peaceful that I wanted to hold my breath. It would have been lovely to have been up in the glen to see the colours of the trees there, we said, but it was nice to be here, too. Very nice. James took me to the sculpture garden where they have sculptures by Henry Moore and Jacob Epstein. And from the edge of the garden we had a fantastic view of Edinburgh, with the castle triumphant in the middle. It was not a bad city: I gave James that.

The day galloped past and soon we were back at Waverley Station, only this time we were not birling and laughing; we were gloomy and quiet.

'Come back for another week-end in a fortnight,' said James. 'Promise!'

'I'll try.'

'It won't be long.'

'No.'

We held hands on the cold platform. People were getting in to the waiting train.

I hesitated, bit my lip, wondered how to say what was on my mind, 'James . . . I'd like to ask you back to my house but – '

'It's all right, I know you haven't the room.'

He could sleep on the settee in the living room, but that would fuss my mother, who was not used to having people to stay, the way Mrs Fraser was. Mrs Fraser fussed, too, but she enjoyed having guests, and both she and Mr Fraser and Grandfather had pressed me to come back as soon as possible. I had had a few good chats with the old boy and we were getting on nicely together. I discovered that he had once made a trip into Central America when he was a student and spent some time with an Amerindian tribe. He had even confessed to me that he would have liked to have spent his life doing things like that, exploring the less well known parts of the world, but his father had expected him to be a lawyer, and so he had. It had been the most sensible thing to do, but he still regretted it, just a little, which did not mean that his life had been unhappy. Far from it.

The guard began to slam carriage doors.

'I'd better go.'

'Okay.'

We kissed, and then I ran from James into the train, clutching my bulging carrier bags.

CHAPTER THREE

I DID not mention the idea of the plumbing business to my family when I returned home. The nearer I got to Glasgow the less feasible did it seem, and all I could imagine was my father's scorn. 'Oh aye, and what'll we use for money, madam? And where do you think we'd find a shop? They don't grow on trees, you know.' I often have conversations with my parents in my head: I can predict so easily what they will say. Sometimes, though, I have to admit, they can surprise me.

The conversation over the Frasers' dinner table faded away into a kind of unreality. It was all right for them to think there was nothing much to going into business, they were used to enterprise, whereas my family had stuck strictly to a line: they signed on and worked for other people. The McKinleys in business? You must be joking.

Another reason I didn't mention it, even jokingly, when I came in, was that my mother had had a turn. She was in the bedroom, and the door was closed. My father was pacing the sitting room floor.

'Your mother's no well,' he said. 'The doctor's with her.'

'What's wrong?' I cried. That sick feeling was back in my stomach.

Apparently she had decided to go and visit my Aunt Jessie. My father had said that he would run her over – and now of course he was blaming himself that he hadn't – but she'd said she'd manage fine on the bus. In a way he'd been quite pleased, for he'd thought it was a good sign that she had been willing to go on her own. So she'd gone and come back, on the bus again, refusing Uncle Tam's offer of a lift. I think she must have been trying to prove something to herself for we'd been going on at her so much. So far, so good. As far as the lift. The lift had stuck between the fourth and fifth floors, with only her in it. She'd panicked, started to scream. She was in there for half an hour before an engineer came and freed her.

It was terrible bad luck.

The doctor gave her a sedative, prescribed more pills. My mother stayed in bed for three days, getting up only to go to the bathroom. She slept and slept. When she did get up and put on her clothes she took care not to look at or go near the windows. In fact, she drew the curtains most of the time and sat under the electric light. And of course she did not go out. The doctor had said that we should try to get her to go into a lift again as soon as possible, but when my father tried to bring up the subject her eyes dilated with terror. I had never seen my mother behave like that before. I was frightened.

I told the Scotts when I went to baby-sit.

'Your father will have to apply for a transfer now,' said Mr Scott. 'He'll have to put in a request for a lower flat.'

'I don't think she'd fancy being in the block at all.

Or any of the blocks. She can't bear to look at them.'

'What about a house?' said Janet.

'There aren't all that many going, are there? And I thought they tended to give them to people with small children.'

'But you could get a medical certificate for your mother,' said Mr Scott.

'Half the women in the block have got medical certificates asking for preferential treatment. They're all going round the bend, eating tranquillisers like Smarties.'

'Now, Maggie, you're exaggerating,' said Mr Scott, who is a great stickler for the exact truth.

'That may be, Colin,' said Janet, 'but you know it *is* a big problem. And a lot of women haven't been able to adapt to high-rise living. It's all right for you men – '

'Yes, yes, I know!'

But he was not being unsympathetic, far from it. He only wanted to look at the problem objectively. And of course everyone, including him, said that it took time to adapt, and five or six weeks was not long enough to give it a chance. My father said so himself and that he didn't like to go to the council and make a fuss yet. 'We'll need to wait for three months to be up,' he said. I told him that might be too late: she might be in a mental hospital by then. That made him uncomfortable, but he wouldn't believe it. She wasn't that bad! I talked a lot of havers at times. One woman in six spends some time as an in-patient in a mental hospital during her lifetime, I informed him; I had recently read an article on mental health. My mother had always been as steady as a rock, my father retaliated, which was not strictly true, for she had had her moments of depression and slight attacks of 'nerves' even in the old place, although he had always done his best to ignore them. He would see about a transfer after three months, he promised, not before; but even then, surely I knew we'd be lucky if we got moved, just like that? He knew of dozens of cases where the woman was on tranquillisers, but they were still sitting on the tenth floor.

Somehow I knew my mother would never take to the high-rise life. She would adapt, yes, i.e. she would never go out. No one, and that included my father, would be able to call that leading a normal life.

'Something will have to be done, Maggie,' said Janet.

'What else can Maggie do if her father won't make a move?' said Mr Scott.

I then mentioned to them the idea of my father and uncle going into business. They did not seem to think it was all that crazy.

'Your family could do with something to alter its structure,' said Mr Scott.

'Shake it out of its rut, you mean?'

'You can hardly get a plumber for love nor money when you need one,' said Janet.

I thought it was unlikely my father would ever go out to work for love, though he would for money.

'Janet's right,' said Mr Scott. 'I don't see how a good plumber could ever be without work. Your father could start in a small way and then move to bigger stuff when he had a bit of capital collected.'

'There are a number of small shops standing empty,'

34

said Janet. 'A lot of little grocers have gone out of business recently, newsagents too. Even round here. . . .' She promised she would keep her eyes open when she went shopping and make a few enquiries for me.

They left to go to the theatre and once the children were asleep I rang James. I had asked the Scotts if I could and they could deduct the cost from my babysitting money. Janet had told me not to be ridiculous. James had told me to reverse the charges when I phoned him since he could not phone me, but I didn't like to in case I got his mother.

Catriona answered and started to yak on about Alexander until I thought I would go crazy. 'Get James for me,' I pleaded. When she put the receiver down Mrs Fraser lifted it and told me how she had begun to do macramé and would I like a belt? I'd love one, I told her, unsure what macramé was. Later I learned it was making things out of string. It sounded suitable for Mrs Fraser. I thanked her for the week-end and she said they had all enjoyed having me, etc. I was jumping up and down by this time: I could hear James's voice in the background now.

'All right, James,' said Mrs Fraser. ''Bye, Maggie.'

At last I was allowed to speak to him! We talked for ten minutes, then he rang me back for another half-hour so that I wouldn't send the Scotts' phone bill up sky-high.

'We can do this every time you baby-sit,' he said.

'Your mother'll have a fit when she sees her phone bill.'

'I'll just have to get a Saturday job to pay for it.'

We laughed, and I realised that the idea of James

getting a Saturday job was simply not on, and could only be a joke. You couldn't imagine him helping in a supermarket, putting tinned beans on a shelf. It made me realise too that there was still quite a gap between us in many ways.

He wanted to know if I was coming the week-end after next and I said that I didn't think I could manage because of *my* Saturday job. It was one of the other pieces of reality I had had to come to terms with on the train. I knew that if I took too many Saturdays off I wouldn't keep the job and couldn't expect to. And I'm not exactly keen on going barefoot through the snow or any of that nonsense.

Now we were depressed. We moaned and groaned across the line to one another and then he said, 'Well, come after work. We'd still have Saturday evening together and all day Sunday. That's better than nothing.'

Of course it was! It was really quite a lot.

But on the Friday of that week-end I had to phone and put my visit to Edinburgh off as my mother was not well enough for me to leave her.

'But she's got your brother and sister, hasn't she?' said James. 'Apart from your father.'

'Sandy and Jean aren't much use. Not at this sort of thing.'

Was I? I wasn't very sure, but she wanted me to stay with her, and so that was enough. My father said I was better than any of the rest of them at taking her mind off herself. That's no doubt because I can usually manage to blether on about something or other. Though that week-end was a test, even for me.

I felt exhausted by the time Sunday evening came.

My throat was sore from talking, mostly to myself. My father nipped out to the football on Saturday afternoon and to the pub on Saturday evening, bringing us back a fish supper apiece as compensation. My mother spent most of the time staring at the wall. She didn't even want the telly on, which was serious. At times I thought I might as well have been declining Latin verbs for all she'd know the difference. I tried to interest her in gossip about some of our old neighbours, resorting to invention when facts were flagging, but the wildest of stories only produced a mild response. It was partly the drugs, I suppose. On Sunday evening Aunt Jessie and Uncle Tam dropped in, which gave me a bit of relief.

Aunt Jessie was wearing a new dress which she paraded up and down for our benefit, then she told us the price and we got a blow by blow account of all the other dresses she had tried on.

'It's real nice, Jessie,' said my mother listlessly.

My father and uncle were drinking beer in the kitchen. Uncle Tam's an easy-going man, jolly, with a red face, and I've never seen him worked up except when Aunt Jessie set their flat on fire half-an-hour before he was due to go and see Scotland playing England at Hampden. It was missing the football match rather than the fire that upset him, you understand.

I went to the kitchen to make some supper.

'Hello there, lass,' said Uncle Tam. 'How're you doing then? Fine eh?'

Only with reservations, I told him, since I was worried about my mother.

'Aye, your dad's said she's no been right. A good tonic'd set her up.'

'Tonic!' I began to slap butter on to bread. Men! They never want to face up to anything. 'Nothing short of getting out of here'll sort her.'

'Ach, she'll settle given time. Nan's aye been one for fussing first.' He is my mother's brother so presumably he should know something about her. Not much though, I considered, when he made statements like that.

'A bit like Maggie herself,' said my father.

They went on smiling and drinking their beer. They couldn't afford to take the idea of my mother in a mental hospital too seriously. It would be far too disturbing.

I put down my knife.

'I want to speak to the two of you,' I said. '*Seriously.*'

They looked up at me, kind of startled.

'I've got a proposition to put to you.'

'What bit of nonsense is in your head now?' said my father.

'Dad, you know you've often spoken about going into business on your own?' I began. He glowered at me as if he'd rather not be reminded, but I continued determinedly. 'Well, I've been thinking about it quite a lot and it seems to me to be a good idea. You couldn't fail – '

'No?'

'All you need is a shop – '

'And money. Which I haven't got.'

'Come off it, you've got a bit put by!'

'A small bit.'

'You wouldn't need a great deal.'

'I've a wee nest egg too,' said Uncle Tam slowly.

'We used to speak of it, Andrew, do you mind? We started saving – '

'That was years ago,' said my father, all gloomy-like. I wanted to kick him. If it had been his mother she'd have been in there pitching, or at least considering the matter. 'This'd be a bad time to start up in business on your own. Look at the state of the economy.'

'There's still work about in our line,' said Uncle Tam. 'We're kept at it. I'm getting tired working for other folk, I wouldn't mind getting a bit of the profit myself for a change.'

I beamed upon Uncle Tam. An optimist, if ever there was one. And an ally for me.

'Oh aye,' said my father, 'it's great talking about profit! But how would we ever get the work to start with?'

'Nothing to it,' I said.

'Is that right?'

'You advertise, do it with a bit of style, attract attention, and after that you just wait for the orders to roll in.'

'Ah aye, you try it then!'

'I would if you'd give me the chance. I could do the advertising, Mum and Aunt Jessie could be recep-tionists in the shop. It'd give Mum an outside interest – '

'Are you serious?' My father stared at me.

'Naturally. Why shouldn't I be? It's quite a feasible proposition.' I was talking myself into it anyway as I went along. 'McKinley and Campbell, Plumbing Engineers!'

'Sounds all right, doesn't it?' said Uncle Tam with a grin.

'Huh! You're both nuts.' My father unzipped another can of beer.

'Dad, you have to take chances sometime.'

'She's right, Andrew. The lass has got go in her, I'll say that!'

'I could say a lot more. Hold your glass up, Tam. Take a drink of beer and come to your senses.'

Uncle Tam took a sip of beer and said, 'D'you know, I wouldn't mind setting up in business? I wouldn't mind at all.'

The more he thought about it the more it appealed to him. Being your own boss. Nobody else calling the tune. My father hummed and hawed and wasn't sure, oh no, he wasn't at all sure. You could get your fingers burnt so easily. He knew dozens who had. We listened to the sagas of their downfalls. A friend of his had started a newsagent's, gone bust after six months, etc. We did not hear of course about any of the success stories. This I pointed out to him, which only made him glare at me for being impertinent.

The door opened, in came Aunt Jessie to see what we were up to. I told her.

'What do you think, Aunt Jessie?'

'Well . . . I wouldn't be all that much against it myself.'

'You see!' I turned to my father. The stick-in-the-mud! I didn't denounce him, not in so many words.

We all went on at him for a bit and in the end he said, 'All right, all right! I'll think about it if Maggie manages to find a suitable shop at a suitable rent.' I had airily said that I would find the premises.

'Okay.' I tried to sound nonchalant, as if it was all but in the bag.

40

A suitable shop at a suitable rent. Quite an undertaking, especially when the terms would have to satisfy my father. On the face of it, it looked quite an impossible task.

CHAPTER FOUR

I BEGAN the search the very next day. After school I went down town and did the rounds of the estate agents. They were not inclined to take me very seriously. I couldn't blame them really, or shouldn't have, though I did. They eyed me, a somewhat scruffy object by the end of the afternoon, decked out in my school gear, and didn't exactly kill themselves in my service. I should have affected a more sophisticated image, worn dark glasses, or ten-foot heels. But I might have had pots of money for all they knew! I put on a Kelvinside accent (posh) and said that my father and uncle were interested in setting themselves up in the plumbing and sanitary engineering business, and did they have any suitable properties on their books?

To buy? No, we didn't wish to buy, not at the moment. To rent.

The rents were extortionate, but I wrote them down in my notebook without blenching, or batting an eyelid, I hoped, said thank you very much and we'll let you know.

I retired to a café in Sauchiehall Street to drink coffee and study the figures. Even the lowest rent would hardly be what my father would call suitable. He expected to be given a shop for next to nothing, or even paid for taking it off someone's hands. I sighed. I didn't feel all that enthusiastic about the search now. Maybe it was a crazy idea. Maybe we should drop it. Then I remembered my mother sitting apathetically in the sitting room with the curtains drawn and knew I couldn't give up that easily. Although if I *did* manage to find a shop it would not automatically mean we'd get living quarters with it. But it would be a start, a new beginning, which seemed to be what was needed.

When I got home I lectured Sandy and Jean on the subject.

'We mustn't just settle down here and let things slide. We can't!'

'What are we supposed to do?' asked Jean.

'Keep your eyeballs skinned!'

'What for?'

'You haven't been listening,' I cried. 'For shops and flats, stupid!'

It was doubtful if Jean would ever find anything, other than the latest pop magazine at the local newsagent's. Sandy might, for he's a sharp lad. He said he'd ask around. He still went back a lot to our old district, had friends there. Not all of it had been knocked to pieces.

'And not a word to Mum about the shop,' I said. 'We won't tell her till it's a *fait accompli*.'

Jean giggled. 'You and your big words, Maggie McKinley!'

'You and your small head, Jeannie McKinley!'

That evening I was due at the Scotts again. I had my fingers crossed that Janet might have found something but she hadn't.

'No luck yet, I'm afraid, Maggie. I've been looking and asking. Thought I'd found something the other day. There's an empty shop round the corner, used to be a newsagent's. I managed to track down the owner, only to find that he'd just signed a lease with someone who's going to start up a hairdresser's. There was a flat above it, too.'

'Oh well! There'll be others,' I said glumly.

'Rotten luck missing that one,' said Mr Scott. 'Good position on the corner, quite a busy road too.'

They went out, I rang James.

'You'll just have to keep looking, Maggie. Don't give up.'

'No.'

'You sound flat.'

So would he if his mother was acting like mine was. I'd had cramps in my tummy in school every time she came into my mind. I told James I was all right, I'd survive.

'I've no doubts about that. Can you come this weekend? Try! Please.'

I would try, I promised, I could put it no higher than that.

My mother was still up when Mr Scott drove me home, my father had just gone to bed. I sat beside her for a few minutes and got round to the subject of me going to Edinburgh for the week-end.

'Would you mind?'

She shrugged.

'I'll stay at home if you want me to.'

'Doesne matter. What's going between you two anyway?'

44

'James and me?'

'Aye. I hope we're not going to give you all this schooling and then you'll just go off and get married.' She still spoke half-heartedly but at least she was speaking, about something. James and me.

I told her that marriage did not interest me, as I had told her on many previous occasions, although clearly she had never believed me, perhaps never would. I had a long and interesting career ahead of me and, besides, it would be seven years before James was qualified. I don't know why parents can't think of things for their children other than the prospects of their getting married. Even Mrs Fraser's mind ran on the matter remarkably often for one who was always harping about preparing oneself for life in the fullest possible way, by which she meant studying and training for a career. She was dead scared that James might 'tie himself down' too soon and that Catriona might marry the wrong person. Like Alexander.

By the time I'd finished describing to my mother the exciting opportunities open to me as a social anthropologist and explaining what a drawback it would be to be married, she was fast asleep, chin on chest, mouth half open. It reminded me of my granny seeing her like that. My mother was looking old, just in these past few weeks. It seemed incredible that she could have changed so much in such a short time. And she was only half the age of my granny. I nudged her awake and led her off to bed, then went myself to mine where I lay, tossing and turning, and hoping for miracles.

I did not go to school in the morning. I borrowed a bicycle from Isobel's sister and set off in search of business premises. It was more urgent than Shakespeare or French grammar.

As Janet Scott had said, there was no shortage of small shops that had closed down. Every time I saw one with its front door shut up and a padlock across, my heart leapt. Then the detective work began. I had to make enquiries, track down the owner. All this quite suited me for I enjoy chatting folk up, going from one lead to the other. I wondered if I might be mistaken in the choosing of a career. Perhaps I should become a private eye? Sleuth McKinley! I stuck my hands deep into the pocket of my raincoat – for, needless to say, it was raining – and walked with a slouch, head bent downwards. It kept the rain off my face at any rate.

All the folk I encountered were ready for a bit of a chat. On such a wet day business was far from brisk. They leant on their counters and confided to me how difficult it was to make a living as a small shopkeeper nowadays.

'I'd think twice if I was you, hen.'

We had thought twice and twenty times I told them, and we were not actually going into the shop-keeping business. My father and uncle were tradesmen.

'Aye that makes a difference right enough. Plumbers do okay. It's not like flogging newspapers and morning rolls.'

Half of the closed shops I made no progress with at all: their owners, if they had any, were untraceable. The other half I found eventually, one way or another, some only at the end of a telephone.

One shop had dry rot, the next wet rot. Was that serious? I asked. Too serious to be let out apparently, until work was done. Some of the shops had been closed compulsorily for not conforming to minimum standards. I couldn't say I was all that surprised from what I could see. Some were up for sale. I found only one for rent.

It was the very end of the afternoon when I found both it and the owner. He lived above, in two rooms. In the half-dark I viewed the crumbling exterior, the slogans scrawled all over the walls. The district was not what James's mother would call salubrious, but would that matter? After all, a plumber went out to people, they did not *have* to come to him, although I had had ideas of making the shop a place of interest, a centre of attraction that would bring in passing customers to buy things like toilet rolls and lavatory brushes.

The man opened the place up. One bare room with a dusty counter at one end. Hardly Harrods! There was a loo in the back premises and a wash-hand basin.

'It'd make a grand wee shop,' he said. 'A lick of paint, and it'd be as good as new.'

He told me the rent and it was reasonable. It would need to be for what was offered. I said I'd think it over, perhaps bring my father and uncle. Bring anyone you like, he said. The thing was that if I'd seen it at the beginning of the day I wouldn't have given it a second look but after the hard facts of reality had struck home I had to be prepared to consider it. *We* had to be, that is.

My father, with a great deal of grumbling, agreed to come and view. He was tired and had been looking forward to putting his feet up. We collected Uncle Tam and drove out to it. I felt as nervous as anything and kept prattling on, telling them how difficult the whole scene was and that we were lucky to get the chance of this at such a low price.

The man descended to let us in. My father viewed in silence. It did not take long. Well, of course there wasn't all that much to see.

'Thanks very much,' said my father. He nodded good-night and we filed out. When we were back in the car he turned to me and said, 'Are you out of your mind or something? What do you think we'd want with a place like that? Nothing more than a slum. Could you see your mother and Aunt Jessie sitting in there being receptionists? And there wasn't room to swing a cat. We'd have stock to house, you know, baths, toilets, basins, copper pipes.'

'All right, all right, so the first place isn't suitable.'

As far as my father was concerned the first place could be the last. He had honoured his side of the bargain and so now he felt he should be allowed off the hook. On the journey back he talked as if that was that. Another of Maggie's stupid notions had bitten the dust. He was even quiet jovial. Relief, I suppose, that he wasn't actually going to have to change his life. My uncle was quiet but when he got out of the car he glanced round at me and winked. I still had an ally. All was not lost!

Not much was gained either, though. I had made a search and drawn a total blank. There would be other days, other parts of Glasgow to search, but I could not take every day off school to look.

My father parked the car, we walked into the

vestibule. I was beginning to hate the place. Bare. Bleak. Concrete. I shivered. Dad pushed the button for the lift, the door slid open.

'I think I'll walk up,' I said.

He looked at me as if I was crazy. Walk up eleven flights from choice? He got in to the lift, the doors closed, and I was left staring at the blank wall. Maybe my mother's phobia was affecting me, too, but I just felt I couldn't face getting into that steel box, watch the doors shut and imprison me. I thought of getting stuck between floors. I'd scream, I was sure I would. After I'd pressed the alarm button of course. It seemed no way to go home, in a box moving upwards, watching the light move up the numbers. Oh, I know thousands – millions – live that way, love it even, or at least some of them do, but I would never be amongst them. We had to get out of this place.

I began my climb. Up and up the grey steps I went, pausing to look down from time to time and see the city lights. At last, puffing and sighing, I reached the eleventh floor. Then, along the straight bare corridor, passing doors behind which other folk lived, but whom I didn't even know by sight, I who had known every single person in my street from the day I was born until we moved out. Why did they have to stack people in compartments like this? To save land? It's not that scarce in Scotland. Mr Scott said they'd gone off the high-rise idea now, decided it didn't work all that well and that people needed closer contact with the ground. That certainly went for us!

My mother was watching telly. She didn't ask where I'd been. She didn't say anything, and then I realised she was sleeping. 'How many of those pills is she taking a day?'

'How should I know?' said my father, who was pretending to read the paper.

'You could count them, dish them out daily.'

'She's not a bairn.'

I went into the kitchen, gazed out of the window. I was restless, couldn't sit. The block across the way stared back at me with its little lit squares breaking its hulk. I'd have liked to go out and walk the streets the way I used to when I felt like this but here there were no decent streets to walk, only a main road running past the scheme, and then one had to go down on the lift to start with. I began to understand why my mother went out so seldom. Once up here you might as well stay.

Next day, at English, I kept yawning my head off, and Mr Scott kept looking at me. After the lesson, he signalled to me.

'Could I have a word with you, Maggie?'

I ambled up to his desk. If he was going to start on me I was going to tell him to lay off. Life was beating me about the head enough as it was.

'You don't have to glare at me like that. I'm not going to eat you.' He was smiling. 'Janet's got some news for you.'

I perked up at once. 'A shop? Not a shop? It couldn't – '

'It could. Why don't you go round and see her after school?'

I did, like a streak of greased lightning. Ran all the way.

'Sit down,' said Janet. 'Get your breath back. I'll make us coffee.'

'Mr Scott said – '

'Did he tell you?'

I shook my head. She sat down.

'Well, you remember I told you about that shop on the corner? I was in the baker's next door today and the woman said that the other deal with the hairdresser had fallen through. So I went back to the owner and he confirmed it.'

'So it's free!' I whooped.

Janet nodded. The flat went with the shop, too. And the rent? Janet told me and my elation petered out a teeny bit for it was kind of high, but she said it was not bad, not for a commercial rent, and one could not expect to get a decent place for much less.

'You don't know my father, though.'

'I'm sure you could talk him into it, Maggie.' She smiled. 'And think how good it would be for your mother. A flat above the shop, other shops nearby, and people going up and down all the time.'

We walked round together to look at it, from the outside. It would be marvellous, really marvellous to live here. No more lifts, long corridors. And this was nearer the centre of town as well.

'It would be great to have you living round the corner,' said Janet. 'The children would be thrilled.'

'Not half as thrilled as I would be,' I said fervently.

I decided that I would approach Uncle Tam first, get him won over, and then together we could face my father.

Uncle Tam hesitated over the rent but agreed

that it probably was fair and as long as they got a reasonable amount of work they should be able to cover it.

'Och aye,' said Aunt Jessie, 'take a chance, for goodness' sake! You'll never get anywhere in this life if you don't.'

She came with us back to the flat. We took Dad into the kitchen, closed the door. He stood with his back against the wall.

'What is this?'

'Third degree,' said Aunt Jessie, with a chuckle.

Between the two of us we bullied him into coming to look. His first reaction, hearing the price, had been: 'Out of the question.'

We made an appointment to view the following afternoon at four-thirty. I could hardly concentrate in school all afternoon, except on the hands of my watch, which moved round with maddening slowness.

We assembled. My father was last to arrive and for the five minutes that we stood there stamping our feet on the pavement I wondered if he was going to chicken out and not come. Then we heard the old car come chugging round the corner.

'It's a good property,' said the owner, as he unlocked the door and ushered us in. He eyed us none too hopefully. My father's face would have been enough to put off a big London property developer.

The shop was a fair size and bare, apart from a scored wooden counter and a dusty glass case at one end. Aunt Jessie ran her hand along the counter. We went into the room behind, which was slightly bigger and could be used for storage and the drinking of cups of tea. A mouse ran across our path and scuttled under the sink, where it disappeared. Aunt Jessie screamed and clutched my arm.

'A cat'd soon clear them out,' said the man.

I noticed a fair pile of mouse droppings in one corner. Well, the place might not have been very Ritz-like but we couldn't expect anything lush, and it did have everything we needed. Also, I realised, it had been a very good thing that we had gone to see that other place, for after it this seemed very, very desirable.

'Plenty room,' said Uncle Tam, whose eyes were agleam. He was beginning to move in. So was I. I was sweeping up the mouse droppings, borrowing Isobel's cat, painting the walls. Aunt Jessie also looked preoccupied, fingering her chin and nodding her head. 'What do you think, Andrew?' asked Uncle Tam.

'It's no bad,' said my father.

'Now the flat,' said the owner.

We had to go outside and up a stair. The flat consisted of four rooms, unfurnished, not particularly large, a kitchenette and small bathroom.

'It's not very big.' My father stood, lips pursed.

'You could manage, though,' said Aunt Jessie. 'Three beds and a sit —'

'I suppose we *could* manage.'

He went through the rooms again with his hands pushed down into his pockets and a large frown cutting into his forehead. You couldn't have said he looked over the moon about it but then he never would about anything, except football perhaps, and only then if his team had won ten nil.

I waited.

'Do you think your mother would like it?'

'Yes! She'd like this street and getting away from the high flats – '

'We'll get away home and see what she has to say about it, then. We might be able to bring her back to see it later.'

We drove home and marched, the four of us, like a deputation into the sitting room, where my mother was watching television. She had her rollers in, had had them in for about three days.

'Would you be quiet, you lot! I'm watching something.'

My father stepped up to the television set and switched it off. She stared at him with astonishment. I could have giggled, but didn't. He stood in front of the set, feet planted apart, and faced my mother.

'Now I want you to listen, Nan.'

She did, protesting at first, saying all the things we had expected her to say, but gradually she grew quiet and you could see her mind beginning to tick over on the good points.

'A shop,' she said. 'A flat.'

'Lovely district,' put in Aunt Jessie. 'Real handy for getting to town.'

'It'd certainly be grand to get out of here,' said my mother slowly.

'Come on, I'll run you over to see it,' said my father. 'Get your coat on.'

'D'you mean now?'

'Why not?' said my father, almost with dash.

Uncle Tam looked at me and winked. My mother began to unwind her rollers.

CHAPTER FIVE

'I WON'T be able to do this very often,' was the first thing I said to James when I alighted from the train at Waverley Station. 'Come to Edinburgh, I mean.' I then went on to explain that my father and uncle were going into business together and that I would have to do a lot of work in the beginning to help them get going. Maggie McKinley *entrepreneur*! Consultant to McKinley and Campbell, Plumbing Engineers! None of us could quite believe it was all happening (not much was yet, except that we had agreed to rent the shop and there was no other topic of conversation in our house), though I was already drawing up a plan of campaign and was hoping that the Frasers might be able to help since they are good on the ideas' front.

James seemed undeterred. He kept on smiling at me and said that was great news. 'I'll come through to Glasgow at week-ends and give you a hand.'

'What do you know about plumbing?'

'As much as you, I imagine.'

He had a point there, though I had learned a lot in the past few days, thumbing my way through plumbing catalogues. It turned out that Mr and Mrs Fraser were not completely inexperienced in the matter for Mrs had once bought a second-hand bathroom suite at a sale and brought it home for Mr to install in one of their two bathrooms. Poor Mr Fraser! The things he get to do. And most of the time he'd rather sit by the fire and read but with a wife like his he has to be sneaky to do what he wants.

Mrs took me to the bathroom to admire the suite and its plumbing. Mr had installed it with her supervising from a do-it-yourself book.

'Maggie does not intend to do any plumbing herself,' said James, who had followed us. 'She is going to do the publicity.' We were filling all available space between the bath, loo and wash-basin. My back felt as if it was going to be cut in half by the towel rail. I had to admire the colour (daffodil yellow) and the pipe joins (or whatever). Anyway, I admired, and was impressed, and then we were released. But at least it did give me the idea of going round the sales in Glasgow to look for second-hand equipment for then we could offer cheaper bathrooms to those who couldn't afford the new prices. Mrs Fraser told me all the things to look out for: chips, cracks, flaws, stains, rough surfaces on the bottom of baths, badly designed wash-hand basins, etc. My head began to reel.

'I'm taking Maggie out for a walk,' said James.

'It's dark,' said his mother. 'And it's damp.'

'They're young,' said Grandpa Fraser. 'A wee bit of damp'll do them no harm.'

We meekly buttoned up our jackets to the throat, at James's mother's insistence, and I was amused at myself, for I wouldn't have done it to please my own mother.

'We don't want to send Maggie home with a cold.'

'I'm tough,' I said, which was not all that accurate. 'And I'm used to the rain.'

'Of course Glasgow is a lot wetter than Edinburgh,' she said.

We walked along Heriot Row in the drizzling rain. It felt fine and fresh against my face and I did not mind it one bit. James said he enjoyed walking in the rain and I said that I enjoyed walking in the rain with him. We laughed at one another, looking up at one another. It was rather nice to be having a break from the subject of plumbing. Absorbing as it was at the moment, I could not see that I would ever want it to dominate my life.

We went through the streets of the New Town, round crescents and squares; we looked at the wet dark dripping trees in the private gardens and through uncurtained windows into lit rooms. I adore looking through uncurtained windows at night and getting little glimpses of other folks' lives. James said I was nosey; I did not deny it.

Of course we were somewhat damp by the time we returned, which made Mrs Fraser tut and shake her head. She hung our coats on the pulley in the warm kitchen and made us hot chocolate to drink in front of the fire.

'How's your granny?' asked Mr Fraser.

I had had a letter during the week from one of her neighbours, a Mrs Clark, who lived upstairs and popped in and out. I fetched Mrs Clark's letter and read it to the Frasers. Granny was doing away nicely, still making broth daily, and on fine days she would take a wee turn around the garden. On bad days she sat by the window and looked out at the hills.

'That's the life right enough,' said Mr Fraser with a sigh, meaning not my granny's in particular, but the life of being amongst the hills, in the glen. 'I'd retire tomorrow and go there if I could.'

'Never mind,' said Mrs, 'we'll be there for New Year. Are you coming with us, Maggie?'

I still had to see which way the wind blew where my family was concerned.

'Of course you've got other things on your mind at present,' said Mrs Fraser.

Like plumbing. Yes.

'I'd like to bring a friend up to the cottage for New Year,' said Catriona in a high voice.

There was a silence in the kitchen. Not even I could think of what to say to break it.

There was no reason why she should not bring Alexander if James was allowed to bring me. Except that they did not like Alexander. And I did not belong to James exclusively, whereas Alexander did to Catriona, for I had made friends with the Frasers all together. But I felt sorry for Catriona and when we went to bed I made myself stay awake for hours listening to her.

'Mother is such a snob,' she said. 'Yes, she is, you can't deny it, can you?'

No, I couldn't. But I supposed most people were snobs in some way or other. Even Catriona. I thought that she should take things a bit more coolly and not try to ram Alexander down their throats so much. It was as if she was deliberately trying to annoy them and

I fancied that if her mother was to take a liking to Alexander Catriona might go off him rapidly. But I wasn't all that sure and I was so tired that I felt myself drifting off irresistibly whilst Catriona was still talking. I slept and dreamt of the glen and my granny sitting by the stove in her old cottage, which existed no longer. The glen was like a strand woven through my life now, and it was for James, too, for he had gone there every year since he could remember. Thus, it formed a bond between us.

I awoke to find sunlight in a corner of the room. I lay feeling drowsy and peaceful, full of warm memories, and from below came the tantalising smell of frying bacon.

There was a tap on the door and James poked his head round. 'Come on, get up, you two lazybones! Breakfast's ready.'

Catriona turned over and growled at her brother. 'I'm not hungry.'

It was amazing that she could not be with such a smell wafting round us. I presumed she was love-sick. Since I was not – sickness is not in my line, it's too boring – I arose and went downstairs where James, his grandfather and parents were waiting to start breakfast. In my family no one would wait for anyone, even if the Queen was coming. She'd have to take her chances along with the rest.

We had bacon, sausages, fried potato scones and eggs, toast and marmalade (home-made of course), and several cups of coffee. I could hardly move when I had finished. My mother says she doesn't know where I put all the food, I'm so skinny.

'Maggie, I've been thinking,' said Mr Fraser, when we had stopped eating. There had been no time to talk whilst we were. 'About publicity for your father's firm.'

My father's firm! How grand it sounded. I sat up a little straighter, insofar as my stomach would allow me.

'And what have you come up with then, Peter?' asked Grandfather Fraser.

'I think we should run off some leaflets on our computer and then Maggie and her family could distribute them in their area.'

'That would be easily enough done,' I said. I had several cousins, and then there were Jean and Sandy and their friends.

'Fine.' Mr Fraser got up and fetched a pad of paper and a pen. 'Let's see if we can compose something suitable.'

We did, on a corner of the table, whilst James and his mother washed up. It read as follows:

McKINLEY & CAMPBELL

PLUMBING ENGINEERS
FIRST CLASS SERVICE
SATISFACTION GUARANTEED
ESTIMATES FREE
BUDGET PRICES TO SUIT EVERY PURSE
24 HOUR SERVICE

So:

If you have any problems
just call us night or day
or visit our showroom at ―

We put the address and telephone number at the bottom, and that was it. During its concoction we had many comments from our observers. Grandfather, with his legal approach, said that it was not possible to guarantee absolute satisfaction; Mr Fraser and I said everyone would know what we meant. Mrs Fraser said it was not possible to offer prices for *every* purse, but we said it was, within reason, and we were not trying to offer anything unreasonable, like getting a new bathroom suite installed for five pounds. Some people, such as Mrs Fraser and Grandfather, have prosaic minds, whereas Mr Fraser and I believe in a little bit of poetic licence. James asked whether my father and uncle would fancy being on call twenty-four hours a day? About that I was not sure, but I thought one of them would have to be (they could take turns during the night) in order to offer something better than the average firm. I foresaw that I might have to do a little bit of arguing and cajoling on this point but, after all, not many loos could flood or drains block during the night. Or could they?

'No, no,' said Mr Fraser. 'It's just so that people feel there's help available round the clock. Come on then, Maggie, let's go up and print it.'

I followed him right up to his study. We ran off a couple of hundred copies.

'If you need more you can always get them photocopied.'

I had a busy week ahead of me. We were getting possession of the shop and flat on Monday, and Sandy and Jean and I were planning to decorate as much as we could before we moved in. I had decided that the shop should be somewhat sensational, and not resemble the normal plumbing affairs with lavatorial colours and a few odd bits of sanitary equipment standing about. I had to admit that a plumbing establishment was not the easiest of places to make attractive – I would naturally have preferred a dress boutique, which would hardly have suited my father – but at least it was a challenge. I was working on a combination of pink, purple and orange.

James rolled his eyes when I told him.

'Just wait till you see it!'

'I'll come on Saturday and help you.'

'Okay.'

I was going to abandon my Saturday job now that I had the family firm to work for. I told my mother so when I returned to Glasgow that evening.

'Honest, Maggie,' she said, clutching her neck with her hand, a habit she has when she is more excited than nervous, 'when I start thinking about it I feel fair sick.'

'It'll all work out just fine, you'll see. You'll enjoy it! You and Aunt Jessie'll have a great time, you can sit and drink cups of tea and blether and take in the orders.'

'I hope there'll be orders to take in.'

Yes, well, so did I. If there were not, I thought I would probably have to head for the hills – of Inverness-shire – to escape the wrath of the McKinley clan.

Her and her big ideas!

CHAPTER SIX

NOW IT was my turn to meet James off a train. He caught the seven o'clock from Edinburgh on Saturday morning and arrived in Queen Street Station in Glasgow three-quarters-of-an-hour later.

'He must be keen,' said my mother, 'getting up at that hour on a Saturday morning.'

'He likes decorating,' said I, innocently.

'Who're you trying to kid?' said Jean.

'Not you, anyway,' I told her. 'I'd be nuts if I wasted my time on such a hopeless cause.' We can still behave like kids to one another without trying too hard.

Jean was all agog at the idea of meeting James. She and Sandy were coming to the shop later in the morning. I had primed them both on all the things they were *not* to say, with little faith that they would even remember, let alone respect my wishes.

When James came through the barrier he was carrying a large canvas hold-all. 'My working clothes. I haven't come to stay. Don't look so worried.'

'I'm not worried. As a matter of fact the Scotts have said you could stay the night with them if you'd like to.'

He said that he would, and then with a grin confided that he had brought his toothbrush, just in case.

'I thought I could always sleep on the shop floor.'

We went into the station buffet and had a cup of coffee before setting off for the shop. I had no idea how many of my relations might have arrived, in spite of the early hour, to gawp at James, so I wanted to have a wee bit of time with him myself. They're a terribly nosey lot, my relatives, and even though I knew they wouldn't ruffle James — he'd just smile peacefully upon them — I knew they'd ruffle me. I have some difficulty at playing things as cool as I think would be desirable for my image, which is that of someone cucumber-like, a trifle bemused by life (you know, with a little knowing smile hovering around the lips) and somewhat distanced from the fray. Instead of which, at moments of crisis, my hair is usually standing on end, my tongue working busily, and my temper bubbles until it finally boils over, and it is only then that I am at peace. From exhaustion.

Over our coffee cups I told James of the progress made. We had distributed the leaflets by putting them through the letter boxes of a random selection of houses. I hoped that one person might tell another. We would become famous by word of mouth.

'Do you think folk sit and talk about plumbers?'

'They might,' said James. I often thought he would say anything to please me so when he tried to reassure me I was not all that reassured.

I had also put ads in two evening papers on two different evenings.

'You've been busy,' said James.

I had also gone to a sale and bought a turquoise bathroom suite, totally lacking in stains, blotches, rough bits, etc., at least as far as my eyes, which are fairly sharp, could detect, and at the same sale had got a carpet for the shop for twenty pounds, two easy chairs for the customers to relax in, and a low table on which I planned to lay out magazines. 'What is it you're setting up?' my mother had wanted to know when I came home and told her. 'A dentist's waiting room?'

'You've been *very* busy,' said James.

'I had to mitch school to go to the sale. Mr Scott found out and he wasn't a bit pleased though he said under the circumstances he'd say no more this time.'

'You mustn't let your work go, Maggie.'

I knew that. I was planning to take six Highers this year. In Scotland we do examinations called Highers a year before they sit A-levels in England, but James, who went to a fee-paying Independent school, was doing English A-levels.

Sandy and Jean and I had almost finished decorating the shop and were planning to start on the flat.

'That's great,' said James. 'I never thought you'd be so efficient, Maggie.'

He was wrong there: I am not efficient, just determined, and if you launch into something like a bull charging you'll probably end up by getting there. At least, that has been my experience.

We left the station and walked out into the sunshine in George Square. The square looked peaceful for it was early yet for many people to be about on a Saturday morning, and there were still a few leaves left hanging brown and yellow on the trees. I wanted very much that Glasgow should look good to James's eyes, that he should like the city and not just see it as a noisy dirty industrial place the way some nit-wits do. It may not be as gracious as Edinburgh – I am willing to concede that – but it does have a kind of zing that makes you feel good to be alive, and the people are friendly and talkative.

'Yes,' said James. 'They *are* talkative.'

We were the only two on the top of the bus. James held my hand. It was mild and sunny for November; we could imagine how beautiful the glen would be with the leaves almost gone and the trees standing slim and bare against the line of the hills. Still, the sun was shining on Glasgow's roofs and James's hand was warm over mine.

When we arrived at the shop there was Sandy dismounting from his bicycle!

'You're early,' I growled, and then introduced them.

Sandy said, 'Hi!' and James said, 'Nice to meet you, Sandy.'

We went inside. The shop sizzled in the morning sun.

'Wow!' said James.

'Do you think it's too much?' I asked anxiously.

'No. It's just – well, it takes a bit of getting used to.'

He paced round the room, eyeing the purple, pink and orange paint.

'It'll look better once the furniture's in,' I said. 'The carpet and chairs are charcoal grey. Either that or they're light grey and filthy.'

'Wait till Mum sees it,' said Sandy. 'She's coming round this afternoon. She'll need an aspirin and a pair of sunglasses.'

'Whatever we would do she wouldn't like it straight

67

off, now you know that.' I was a little uneasy about the strength of the colour, but I was not going to admit it for I couldn't face trying to paint over any of it, not after all that effort.

'Well, let's get to work,' said James, who was raring to go. Sandy and I were less keen since we had been painting every evening that week and had the smell in our nostrils even when we woke in the mornings.

James changed into a pair of paint-stained jeans and an old shirt. He had brought his own brushes, too. He had thought of everything, or his mother had.

'Maggie,' he said, 'I think you should paint the woodwork white. That pink is just a little bit much, don't you think?'

'I don't know.' I was feeling mulish. I had already done the undercoat and bought the top coat.

'You could use the rest of the pink in the flat somewhere, in the bathroom perhaps.' He rummaged in his canvas hold-all and brought out a large can of white gloss paint. 'Present from Mother.'

'Oh, okay.' I gave in with bad grace, but half-an-hour later I told him I thought he was probably right after all and he winked at me.

Sandy sat on the window-sill, yawning, with his transistor playing beside him. I told him there was no point in his coming if he was just going to sit there.

'She's a real slave-driver, you know,' he said to James. 'She'd drive you till you dropped.'

'That's not true.' I was furious, for half the time I'm not doing anything all that energetic myself. My energy comes in bursts. This week had certainly seen an explosion, and I could hardly get to sleep at nights with my mind ticking over on all the things to be done.

Jean arrived with her friend Lorraine. They giggled and eyed James as if he'd stepped out of some pop magazine. He had only come from Edinburgh for goodness' sake! And he was nothing special. Well, maybe he was to me, but that was no reason for them to behave as if he'd come from a different planet and wasn't able to see or hear them, either.

'Why don't you two go and buy some rolls and make us all coffee?' I suggested.

'Maggie never thinks of anything but her stomach,' said Jean.

'Well, it's thin enough,' I snapped. 'Which is more than I can say for yours.' Jean was a little plump. She blushed, and as she and Lorraine turned to go she stuck her tongue out at me.

'Younger sisters are a pain,' I said to James.

He agreed. 'Though you're always telling me I shouldn't say that Catriona is.'

'Why is everybody annoying me this morning?' I demanded.

The door opened to admit a swirl of wind, a few dry leaves, and Uncle Tam and Aunt Jessie.

'Mercy me!' cried Aunt Jessie.

'What's the matter?' I asked.

'The colours! I'll never be able to sit with yon colours round me all day, Tam. You ken I like pastel shades. Pale blue and cream would have been awful nice.'

'You'll get used to it, Aunt Jessie.'

Then she noticed James, and her manner changed. She advanced towards him, all smiles, her hand out ready to take his. 'Is this your young man then, Maggie? Oh I am pleased to meet you.'

I ground my teeth together and counted to ten, and wished, not for the first time, that I had been born into a totally different outfit. Or was orphaned, and totally lacking relations.

Jean and Lorraine returned with the rolls and made coffee on the gas ring in the back shop. We sat on the window-sills and counter to eat and drink.

'I hear you're coming out to be a doctor?' Aunt Jessie said to James. She couldn't take her eyes off him.

'I hope so.'

'That's lovely.' She smiled at him and he smiled at her. It was too much for me. I took my cup through to the back shop to rinse and as I departed I could hear her telling him how smart I was at school and how I'd learned to read before I was four. . . . I closed the door firmly behind me and ran the water noisily so that I would not have to hear another word.

The door opened, and James appeared with his cup. He was grinning away as if he was enjoying himself.

'Your family are very proud of you, Maggie.'

'Huh!'

'But they are.'

'Wait till you meet my mother. She'll tell you a different story.'

But when my mother arrived in the afternoon she only said, 'Pleased to meet you,' to James, as gentle as a lamb. After that she goggled a bit at the walls and had to take a seat. I had brought in one of the armchairs in anticipation.

'Trust you!' she said at length, but her words lacked

the force that would have been there if James had not been present. 'Your Aunt Jessie and I'll be dizzy as two tops when we get out of here each day.'

'I'm putting up white curtains,' I said. 'That'll soften it.'

'Curtains? In a plumber's shop?'

'It looks like some fancy hair salon,' said my father, who so far had not spoken to James but had merely nodded to let him know he had seen him. He stood now in the centre of the shop feet planted apart, brow furrowed as if he'd suddenly been made President of the United States.

'Mind you,' said my mother, 'it is different, and as Maggie says, you have to do something different if you're to get on in business.'

'Don't you encourage her!' said my father. 'She's bad enough without being encouraged.' He turned to me. 'Folk don't often come into plumbers' shops, anyway.'

'They will to this one by the time we're done. I thought we could sell all sorts of things on the side, hardware, kitchen stuff, and Jean's great at making soft toys. We could do a good line in them for Christmas.'

'You see,' said Aunt Jessie to James, 'isn't she a clever wee lass?'

'Very clever,' said James.

Jean made us all a cup of tea and produced a tin of home-made shortbread, made by herself. She'll make someone an ideal wife, that is for sure. My mother is always saying so. Unlike me. She's always saying that too, though not today with this blond stranger from that other city in our midst. As she drank her tea she eyed him covertly, where he sat on the end of the counter with his long legs dangling. He was much taller than anyone in my family.

Aunt Jessie followed me into the back-kitchen this time. 'You're doing all right, Maggie,' she said in the kind of hoarse whisper that can be heard at the other end of a football pitch.

'What do you mean?'

She nudged me in the ribs. 'He's got real class.'

We went back into the shop to find that my father, Uncle Tam and Sandy were on the point of departing. They were off to the football.

Uncle Tam hesitated, looked at James. 'Are you wanting to come with us? To the football like?'

'No, no thanks. I'll stay and help Maggie.'

'Do you never go to the football?'

'Well – '

They awaited his answer. They would find it difficult to believe him if he were to say no, and James, sensing that, obviously, said not very often, whereas I doubted if he had ever been to a football match in his life. He played rugby.

The football fans went. Aunt Jessie took my mother away; they were going downtown to have a look at the shops. It was wonderful to see my mother taking an interest in life again. Knowing that we were leaving the high-rise had done more for her than ten bottles of pills ever would have. As was only to be expected, Jean and Lorraine vanished, giggling, to keep some secret assignation, and James and I were mercifully left alone.

'Thank goodness!' I said. 'Now we can get on with the important business. All they do is keep you back.'

'Do you think they approved of me?'

I turned to him in surprise and saw that he meant it: he really did want to know if they liked him, and cared whether they did or not.

'Yes, they approved.' I grinned.

'Not your father, though?'

'He's just suspicious by nature.'

'A bit like you, eh?'

I could have thrown the pot of paint at him for I prided myself that I had none of my father's reactionary attitudes.

'You were suspicious of us in the beginning,' said James. 'Weren't you?'

I told him it was mean to refer back to the past. Well, I might have been a little cagey where the Frasers were concerned, but they had been a bit overwhelming with all their ruddy health and hill walking and emphasis on the 'good life'. I had not been used to that kind of thing.

'Exactly.'

He came and kissed me, which softened and soothed me, and then we went back to work. We finished the shop and started on the sitting room in the flat.

The football fans returned after the match. They had faces as long as your arm on them so we didn't need to ask who'd won. They were still arguing about who should have been dropped from the side and who should have been picked. They discussed, blow by blow, each step of the game.

'You didn't miss anything, James,' sighed Uncle Tam. He looked round. 'You're fairly getting on here.'

'Are you wanting any help?' asked Sandy in a voice that lacked enthusiasm.

I said we could manage without him if he had other fish to fry. But that reminded me I was hungry. We were going to have a meal at the Scotts' later, James and I, but I felt a bit peckish in the meantime.

'Not again,' groaned Sandy. 'Oh all right. I'll go out and get you some fish and chips.'

My father took some money from his pocket and gave it to him. 'Get them chicken suppers if they want them. We'll be off then, Maggie. See you later.' He nodded to James.

'James is staying till tomorrow, Dad.'

'Oh? That's fine.' He did not sound as if he quite meant it but, on the other hand, he did not sound displeased, either. I am fairly good at measuring my father's moods and half the time I think he's not sure what he feels about something. Like me!

James and I ate chicken and chips with our fingers, and James said that he was also beginning to wonder where I put all the food. I burn it up, I told him, by generating brain power.

We worked for another two hours or so, by which time we were tired and had had enough of painting that day. James told me to sit down whilst he cleaned the brushes and tidied up. I hate all that part of decorating. We have a number of old brushes as stiff as pokers to testify to that.

We washed, changed and locked up the shop. The night was nippy but clear with a big rash of stars spread above the rooftops. People were going up and down the street, couples mostly, off for a Saturday night out.

I like the movement of people and cars, especially at evening when the lights are lit. The city seems more mysterious and exciting then.

The Scotts were waiting for us in their warm snug sitting room. Here I could relax for I did not have to worry that either of them would start making embarrassing personal remarks about me, except for the children who did not matter. They came down in their dressing-gowns to see James and asked, 'Is Maggie your girl-friend?' and 'Do you like her?'

They were chased away to bed by Janet, and Mr Scott poured us a glass of wine. They had a big log fire roaring in the grate, which smelled delicious and felt gorgeous after a day in the unheated shop.

James was at ease with them at once. He and Mr Scott chatted away about all sorts of things; I got up and went to the kitchen to see if I could help Janet, which I knew I couldn't, but I leant against the draining board and watched her making a sauce to go with the meat. The smell coming from the oven was making me drool.

'What do you think of James?' I asked.

She thought he seemed nice. I had known that she would.

CHAPTER SEVEN

McKINLEY & CAMPBELL, Plumbing Engineers, opened their premises to the public the following Saturday morning. We were not exactly swamped by the public but McKinleys and Campbells were there in strength. The only members of the public to appear, in fact, were the Scotts, apart from James, who could scarcely be counted. He arrived on the same early morning train, carrying his hold-all. In it he had another pot of paint. Wedgwood green this time, sent by his mother. She had thought it would be nice for my bedroom.

'We should have had champagne,' I said. 'And broken a bottle against the door for the launching.'

'I could go and buy a bottle of coke,' offered one of my younger cousins.

We had neither coke nor champagne but instant coffee, accompanied by chocolate fudge cake which Jean had made for the occasion.

'She's a grand wee baker,' said Aunt Jessie, licking her fingers. She was still eyeing James one week later. 'Maggie's quite handy that way too, aren't you, hen?'

'I'm hopeless, and James knows it.' The 'hen' was the last straw: I hate that particular Scottish endearment.

I saw James smothering a laugh. He said, 'It's certainly a fine cake.'

'You've made a grand job,' said Aunt Jessie, meaning the decorating of the shop and that it was James who was responsible.

'Oh, I only did a little bit,' he protested.

I left them to it and pushed my way through to the door, where I had caught sight of Janet Scott.

'We thought we'd come and see how it was going.'

'Come in. If you can get in.'

Some of the young Campbells were playing tag in and out of the crowd. I caught a couple by the scruff of the neck and put them outside, then I gave them fifty pence to go to the corner shop.

The Scotts admired our decor and thought we had done very well indeed.

'I adore pink, purple and orange together,' said Janet. 'All hot and sizzly. Gorgeous!'

I turned triumphantly to my father, who was beside us, but it would take more than Janet's approval to impress him.

'You canne see it properly for all the folk,' he said. 'They hide the worst of it.'

Janet laughed. 'You're not a man for colours then, Mr McKinley?'

'No when they roar at you.'

'He's just like his mother,' I said a bit snappily, for it was true. His mother, my glen granny, couldn't abide bright colours, and favoured brown, beige and sludge green. 'But she's eighty-three.'

'She was aye the same.'

'It's about the only way you two are alike,' I told

him, and then I folded up that conversation so that I could introduce my father to Mr Scott. 'Mr Scott's my English teacher, Dad.'

'I'm right sorry for you, Mr Scott,' said my father. 'She canne be easy to have in a class.'

'No, she's not,' said Mr Scott.

'I expect you find she canne keep her mouth shut?'

'I do.'

'She's the same in the house. Aye telling us all what to do.' It was amazing how talkative my father was this morning. Starting up as a business tycoon must have been going to his head.

'She sometimes tries to tell me what to do,' said Mr Scott. He smiled at me. 'Usually without success, I must admit.'

Charming!

'Don't listen to them, Maggie,' said Janet.

'I'm not.'

'You're Colin's star pupil.'

'I don't know what the rest can be like then,' said my father. I stared at him, wondering if he had had a dram for breakfast for it was not like him to crack jokes, especially amongst strangers.

I took Janet off to show her the rest of the premises.

'The place is looking great, Maggie. I'm so pleased I saw it.'

'So am I.'

Janet bought a few of the items on display: tooth-brush holder, lavatory brush, scouring powder, four rolls of toilet paper and a bottle of bath essence.

'You don't have to buy anything, Janet,' I said.

'But I need all these things. Honestly!'

It was fine anyway to ring up the first sale on the till. Everyone stopped talking and turned their heads when they heard it.

'It's a grand sound that,' said Aunt Jessie.

'Let's hope it never stops,' said Uncle Tam.

'Time will tell,' said my mother.

'Aye, well, it'd better no take too long telling,' said my father, 'for Tam and I have given up our jobs and we've no more wages to come now.'

My father had also exchanged his car for a van, which was equally ramshackle but would cart the basins and loos and pipes around.

'We just need a wee snap of cold weather and there'll be plenty of burst pipes,' said Uncle Tam, who is more optimistic by nature than my father, which would not be difficult.

The Scotts decided that they must go, they had all the weekend shopping to do. James and I accompanied them to the door.

'Well, all the best for the shop, Maggie!' said Janet.

'And for your English essay due in on Monday,' said Mr Scott.

It was a pity one could not make faces at one's teachers even on a Saturday morning. I allowed myself a mild groan.

'See you later, both of you,' said the Scotts, and away they went with their children between them, laden with toilet rolls. James was to spend the night at their house.

My young cousins were playing hopscotch on the pavement in front of the shop.

'Give us a go,' I said, and they did. I hopped up

and down, my feet zigzagging and scissoring, between the chalk marks. 'Come on,' I cried to James. He began to follow me, a bit awkwardly at first, but soon his legs became smooth and sure and the kids yelled and cheered and we all ended up breathless and laughing.

'That was fun.' James pushed the lock of hair back from his forehead.

'Didn't you play at hopscotch when you were a kid? Or is Heriot Row too grand for that?'

'The neighbours aren't too keen on having their pavement chalked on.'

One of the girls was skipping and singing. 'One, two, three-a-leerie. . . . Four, five, six-a-leerie. . . .'

She gave me her rope. I hadn't skipped for ages but it's one of those things you never forget. Soon the rope was flying under my feet and the kids were chanting:

> 'In a castle on a mountain
> Lives a man called Frankenstein.
> And his daughter Pansy Potter
> Hopes to get a valentine.'

'What in the name are you doing now, Maggie McKinley?' asked my mother, who had come out of the shop with Aunt Jessie. 'Will you never grow up?'

'I sure hope not.'

Aunt Jessie gave me a disapproving look to warn me that was not the way to carry on in front of 'my young man'. I really should try to look a bit more dignified!

'We're off to the shops,' said my mother. 'We have to get the lunch ready for the men.'

'So that they can go to the football on time,' I said.

'It's all right, James and I will look after the shop and record all orders carefully.'

The McKinleys and Campbells dispersed; James and I cleared up, removing sweet wrappers and cigarette ends, washing cups and saucers. Then we sat down behind the counter and waited. The scarlet telephone sat silent in front of me. Upstairs in the flat we had an extension. It was the first time we had ever had a phone, and my father had duly warned me that I was not to blether on it for hours, he couldn't afford to foot the bill, and so on.

'You can't expect anything to happen today,' said James. 'Not the first day.'

'No, I know.' But there was nothing wrong with hoping, was there? James agreed that there was not but said it would be silly to be disappointed if one did not get an order the first day, or even the first week. The first week! I looked at him in horror at the very idea, for my father would go off his head. He liked his security, needed it, and was not one for going off gold prospecting into the unknown or anything like that. I could have imagined my granny doing it before he ever would, for she had in her the blood of her granny, who had been brave and full of courage, carrying a dying sister through the mountains after they had been evicted at the time of the Clearances in Scotland.

'I'd like to go to Greenyards,' I said. 'And see where my great-great-granny came from.'

'Yes, let's!'

The phone rang. I leapt to it and had the receiver in my hand before the second ring. It was a wrong number!

'Why don't we have some lunch?' suggested James. 'Or aren't you hungry today?'

I had actually forgotten about my stomach. James stayed in the shop whilst I went out and bought some sausage rolls and crisps and two large squashy cream cakes. We picnicked on the counter, and I was licking the last of the cream from my fingers when I was aware of someone darkening the doorway. Glancing up, I saw Mrs Fraser on the other side of the glass door.

'Mother!' said James.

She came in, followed by Mr Fraser and Catriona.

'We thought we'd come and see your shop, Maggie!'

'It looks terrific,' said Catriona.

'It certainly does,' said Mr Fraser.

Mrs Fraser had a look in the corners to see if we'd missed anything, but in the end gave us her nod of approval and told us we had made a good job of it.

James was less pleased by their arrival than I was – I thought it very nice of them to come all that way – but I could understand his reaction for I would have felt the same if my mob had turned up at his place in Edinburgh. I made them coffee, could offer no food for we had scoffed the lot but that did not matter since Mrs Fraser had come prepared. Mr Fraser unpacked from the car a hamper containing stacks of sandwiches, bags of fruit, and a tin of newly baked flies' cemeteries. I was persuaded to join them but James said that he was not hungry. He sat in the corner, looking slightly sulky and quite different from what he had been in the morning. Folks' moods don't bother me, so I just let him get on with it. There was nothing I could do about it anyway and I was enjoying telling Mrs Fraser and Catriona all the ins-and-outs of my week in the publicity and plumbing world. I also showed them material I had bought for curtains for our new sitting room and Jean's and my bedroom. Jean had promised to make them for I am nowhere when it comes to wielding a needle. Or, as my mother would say: I don't try.

'We're just about broke now,' I said, as I rewrapped the material. 'I've even spent money I'd saved for a new winter jacket.'

James got up. 'I think I'll go and do some painting upstairs, Maggie.' He picked up the pot of Wedgwood green paint and left.

'D'you know, Maggie,' said his mother, 'I wouldn't mind a wee walk to stretch my legs before we go back. Is there anywhere round here we could go, a park maybe?'

There was a park not far away, a small one, but that would do, she said. She wanted me to go with her.

'But I have to look after the shop.'

'Catriona can do that. And Peter can give James a hand.'

It was then that I realised that she wanted to get me on my own, to have a 'little talk' with me.

We walked up the street and were inside the park gates before she approached the subject.

James. Well, I had known that must be it. What else? She was worried about him, he was not studying as much as he ought, or as he used to. And the reason? That was easy to find. I objected, saying that this was only the second week-end he had come, but of course Mrs Fraser wanted to nip it in the bud before it got out of hand. She said that James really could not continue to come to Glasgow every week-end, for if he did he might end up by not doing well enough in his A-levels to get a place at medical school. And I would not want that, would I? What questions some people ask!

'So you see, Maggie,' she went on, 'I must ask you not to encourage him to come too often. He could come through the odd Saturday, for the afternoon, but I think anything more is out of the question. If you come up to the glen with us for New Year you'll see one another then. After all, you are both very young and you can't expect to be at all serious about one another, can you?' She gave a laugh which she meant to be light and tinkly but dropped like a suet pudding.

'What do you mean by serious?' My stubbornness was building.

'Well. . . .' She laughed again, then sobered fast. 'I think you and I know one another well enough now to be able to talk frankly, don't you, Maggie?'

'I suppose.'

She started to talk about James having seven years of study ahead, and then he might specialise, he was interested in pediatrics, etc. I knew all that. What she was saying was that he could not think of getting married in less than about ten years' time by her reckoning.

'Mrs Fraser,' I said, interrupting her, 'do you think *I* want to get married? I'm only sixteen.'

'No, I'm sure you don't, at least not at the moment, though some girls do – '

'I am not *some* girls.'

'But since you can't hope for anything like that for a very long time I think it might be wise if you don't get too intense about one another, that's all.'

'I think it's difficult to promise not to be intense in any situation.' I felt I was being very cool and mature, I was not letting her ruffle me, for in a way I was more in control of the situation than she was. It seemed a ridiculous conversation for me to be involved in.

'The only way is not to see one another too much.' It was a bit like Victorian times. Part for one year or else forever! 'After all, you've got your own school work too,' she added.

I had, and I also recognised that James must not allow his to slip, either. I sighed. Life had seemed so rosy this morning and had promised an endless stream of Saturday mornings of rising at the crack of dawn (what a thing for me to come to!) to go down to Queen Street Station whilst most folk were still sleeping, and wait for James's smiling face to appear in the train window. But it looked as if we were not going to be able to continue as we would have liked. It burns me up when something's going nicely and then you have to give it up, or partly, for reasons that you can't kick against.

'You're young, Maggie,' said Mrs Fraser again, making me want to scream. If she had been my own mother I would have done.

I promised that I would not encourage James to come too often to Glasgow, and also that I would not tell him that his mother had spoken to me.

'He wouldn't like it, you see, dear.'

That was one of the understatements of the year.

We left the park. I hoped my halo was shining for the world to see. McKinley the self-sacrificing saint!

There had been no telephone calls and no personal callers either, Catriona informed us on our return. Her father and brother were working busily in my bedroom upstairs, making the walls a pretty green.

'That should look nice and fresh,' said Mrs Fraser brightly, but I was not feeling very warm towards her right then, so I refused to give her any satisfaction by agreeing.

I went back downstairs to see Catriona and hear the latest on Alexander.

'Your mother must be doing her nut worrying about you and James and your love lives.'

Catriona giggled. 'I think she'd like to lock us up until we were of sound mind. Whenever that might be!'

My mother and Aunt Jessie reappeared before the Frasers left.

'I'm so pleased to meet you, Mrs McKinley,' said Mrs Fraser, with too much gush for my mother. 'I've heard so much about you from Maggie here.'

My mother glanced at me with suspicion. I widened my eyes innocently.

Aunt Jessie said, 'We're awful pleased to meet you too, Mrs Fraser. We're all getting right fond of your James. He's getting to be like one of the family you could say, couldn't you, Nan?'

Nan said nothing. We stood about with Aunt Jessie and Mrs Fraser smiling at one another, the rest of us shifting from foot to foot.

'Well, I think we should be off,' said Mr Fraser. 'I'd just as soon do the drive in daylight.'

'Quite right,' said Aunt Jessie. 'Yon's a busy road.

And the accidents these days. . . .' She shook her head. She is very fond of accidents is Aunt Jessie, relishing all details, and every time I see her she usually has one for me. Not that I want it. But one gets a lot from relatives one doesn't want.

'See you soon, Maggie,' said Mrs Fraser, and to James, 'Don't be too late home tomorrow now. Remember you've got your maths to finish and – '

'Yes, all right.' He was impatient.

We waved them off.

'Your mother and father are awful nice,' said Aunt Jessie to James. 'It was real good of them to come all this way just to see our Maggie.'

CHAPTER EIGHT

THE WEEK that followed was not one of the best that I can remember. On the Sunday evening, before we parted at the station, James and I were depressed at the prospect of saying goodbye for a few weeks. I had told him earlier that neither of us could afford to spend our week-ends doing this and he had reluctantly agreed, even with some relief, I suspected, for I knew he did want to do well in his exams and get to university, and perhaps he had been worried about not working enough. He had told me once that he was not brilliant but he could get there by plodding. No doubt his mother knew best! A horrible thing to have to concede.

The essay I handed in to Mr Scott on Monday morning was not one of my best either, and I did not need him to tell me that, though he did, without mincing his words. Mr Scott is no word-mincer, ever. That may be why we get on so well together.

'Maggie,' he said, 'at times you can do work that is absolutely brilliant, much better than anyone else's; it really sings. At other times you can turn in the most appalling rubbish.'

It was not surprising that that particular essay was of the appalling rubbish variety for I had written it in bed at eleven o'clock on Sunday evening after an exhausting week-end of painting, and James, and family. No, families, for although the Frasers only hit Glasgow for two to three hours, they left their mark. At least Mrs did. Her little talk had had the effect of dropping me to the lower depths, and after I had scrawled my essay and put the light out I lay awake, thinking about what she had said and wondering if the sanest thing to do might be to stop seeing James altogether. But then I am not noted for my sanity.

I had fallen asleep somewhere in the revolting hours of three or four o'clock and my mother had had the devil's own job to get me awake enough in the morning to stagger to the bathroom to wash my face. The school bell had gone before I arrived, which meant a blast from my form teacher who had already marked me absent.

Then she looked at me.

'Are you feeling all right, Maggie?'

I had no doubt that I would be looking like death walking, for I usually do after a bad night, or when I'm ill, for I have a sallow skin, almost lacking in any tinge of pink except when the Frasers have dragged me up a hill in the teeth of a force ten gale.

'Not really,' I said in a faint voice.

She sent me to lie down in the medical room, on a settee with a hot-water bottle and a tartan travelling rug over me. I dozed the morning away beautifully and emerged quite fresh at lunch-time. Unfortunately our English period was in the afternoon so I did not escape having to hand in my essay. I escaped Mr Scott's wrath until the following day since he had no chance to glance at it before I fled.

'It's all very well helping in the family business, Maggie, it's very commendable and all that, but you have to remember your own work comes first. It would be a great disappointment to me and other members of the staff if you didn't do well in your Highers.'

'That's all very well, but we have to eat at home too, you know. A fat lot of good six Highers'll do me if our business goes down the drain.'

'I know all that, and I sympathise. It's not easy.'

No, it was not, especially since we were flitting the following day (moving house, in case you don't know), and my mother had said I would have to stay at home and help. Sandy and Jean needed their schooling more than I did – I was smart enough – and she could not manage alone.

'But you'll have Dad and Uncle Tam. It's not as if they've got any other work to do.'

That was not the thing to have said since it started her off lamenting and complaining so, to cut it short, I agreed I would stay. My father is useless when it comes to any kind of domestic work anyway, and I supposed my mother would want me for moral support as well. She was very much better but her 'nerves' were not quite settled. She was still slipping the odd pill into her mouth, though she claimed she'd given them up entirely. I had hidden one bottle but discovered that she had a reserve supply.

She said I could tell my form teacher I had had a bad headache. My form teacher was suspicious of my headaches so, when it came to the point, I told her a long garbled story about my mother and her nerves, high flats, the plumbing business and the troubles of flitting. At the end of it the poor woman did not quite know what to believe so contented herself by warning me not to do it too often. I assured her that I would not. When I saw Mr Scott coming along the corridor I ducked round the corner and waited until he had passed. So, one way and another, it was a tiring week and I did not achieve very much schoolwise.

My mother and Aunt Jessie took it in turns to sit in the shop, though often they sat together for they liked the company. They chatted and watched the passers-by.

'Not much else to watch,' said my mother.

They sold two lavatory brushes, four tins of scouring powder and a number of toilet rolls.

'We'll no live very well off the sale of toilet rolls,' said my mother.

'Give it time,' I said. 'James said it'd take a week or two to get going.'

'Aye, he's right,' said Aunt Jessie. 'Smart lad that one.'

On Thursday a woman needed a new washer on her sink tap.

'A washer!' said my mother.

'Never mind,' I said. 'Big businesses start in small ways.'

'I'm no caring about being in big business,' said Aunt Jessie. 'Just as long as we have enough to buy our butcher meat and pay the electric and a few wee things like that.' Even she, normally so even-natured, was getting a little bit edgy about the whole thing.

That evening I was baby-sitting for the Scotts.

'Nice to see you for a change,' he said sarcastically.

I moaned and groaned to them about the state of

affairs, but they said to that we must not expect immediate results and that we might have to sit it out for a few weeks.

'A few weeks,' I echoed.

My father's savings were dwindling, as was his patience.

The next morning Janet called the shop and asked if they could plumb in her automatic washing machine. When I came home and heard about it I was furious and rushed round at once to see her.

'But, Maggie, I've been meaning to have it done for ages. I've kept having to fill it and drain it from the sink and it's been such a pain. Really!'

I calmed down. I could see that it was like her to have kept putting something like that off so I supposed it did not really matter that she was having the job done now partly to help us out. She had also arranged for my father to put in plumbing for a dish-washer. They were only small jobs, of course, that would scarcely pay the rent but they were better than nothing. Janet also had a friend along the street who wanted a new wash-hand basin in her bathroom as one of her children had dropped a glass jar of bath salts into her old one from a great height.

James phoned me twice that week and I phoned him once. He said, 'I wish I was coming to Glasgow this week-end,' and I said, 'I wish I was coming to Edinburgh,' for I was beginning to feel I could do with a break from plumbing and my mother's reproachful face. My father was not saying much but he went to the pub a bit more than usual, which did nothing to help my mother. I got Jean started on making soft toys, which she does very well, and she made some really cute ones, pink elephants, green sausage dogs and some rusty-red cats. We put them on sale on Saturday at very reasonable prices, much lower than you would normally pay for things like that, and sold out before lunch-time. Jean was 'fair away with herself', as we say in Scotland.

'Pity I can't sew faster,' she said. 'Pity you can't help, Maggie.'

I groaned. 'Don't you think I have enough to do?' During the course of the week-end I was planning to decorate the bathroom, look after the shop, write a history essay, do a long piece of French translation and read a couple of books that I should have read the week before.

'Why don't you get Lorraine to give you a hand?' I suggested. 'She's quite good at sewing too, isn't she? We could even pay her something per hour, a small something of course. Dad'd have a fit if he thought I was paying out wages!'

I sat at the counter and did the books for the week. It didn't take long! Then I decided what we should order in the way of toilet rolls, etc. It seemed that one could always sell these and I thought that it was a good idea for people to form a habit of coming regularly into the shop so that when they did need a plumber they would think of us.

'Aye, that's fine, lass,' said Uncle Tam, 'but what we really need is one or two big orders, like replumbing a house, installing a new bathroom, things like that.'

'It'll come,' I said, though I feared the conviction in my voice was steadily weakening.

Janet came in in the afternoon, having heard that we had been selling the toy animals.

'I'd like a couple for the kids for Christmas.'

'Okay. I'll take your order.'

I got a notebook and wrote 'Christmas Orders' on the front, and by evening had taken quite a few.

My old friend Isobel came in around tea-time. 'Nice place you've got here, Maggie,' she said. She had a seat in one of the armchairs, I made some coffee and we had a blether.

'What about coming out tonight, Maggie? All the old crowd's getting together. We're going to a disco.'

'I can't, Isobel, I've got too much to do.'

'But it's Saturday night. Do you never go out and enjoy yourself these days?'

I told her that I did but could see that she did not believe me. She would never have understood that I was actually enjoying myself in the shop, or when I went baby-sitting, and at school too. One thing I was not enjoying was not seeing James. It was difficult to concentrate on history that evening when I thought that I might have been with him, laughing and talking, walking through the streets with my hand in his. I stayed on in the shop doing my homework with the curtains drawn. It was quiet there with no one to disturb me. Jean and Sandy were out, my mother and father were upstairs watching television.

When the phone rang it startled me for I was sitting with my chin on my hand, my elbow on the counter, thinking of James.

'Hello,' said James.

'I was just thinking about you.'

'That's nice. I've been thinking about you all day. Are you alone?'

He was alone too; his parents had gone to the theatre, his grandfather was dining with a friend, and Catriona was out with Alexander.

'It seems crazy that we are sitting separate and alone,' he said, 'and that we can't be together.'

'We are being sensible,' I told him. It was such a strange thing for me to be that I began to wonder how it had come about.

We talked for an hour, about school, the Scotts, our families, and came back, as always, to the glen. It beckoned to us like a haven of peace where we could have wandered without thinking about time or exams or being sensible.

'I'll ring you next,' I said. 'Goodbye, James.'

'Goodnight, Maggie.'

It was awfully quiet and lonely in the shop after I had put down the receiver. I had to go upstairs to the warm sitting room and sit with my mother and father for a few minutes. They were watching an old film. I flopped down on to the settee beside my mother.

'Don't be working too hard now, Maggie,' she said. 'You're looking tired. Isn't she, Andrew?'

'She's never in her bed till all hours,' he said, without taking his eyes from the screen.

I yawned.

'Away to your bed now, lass,' said my mother.

'I've got a history essay to finish.'

'That can wait till the morn.'

She was right: it could, and sometimes things are better left to morning. I went to bed and slept at once and dreamt of James and my granny's glen. It was a recurring dream now, and I was beginning to look forward to it as I got ready for bed.

In the morning I wrote my history essay without pausing; my mind was clear and my pen moved fluently. At the end of it I knew I had done a good piece of work and was pleased.

We had an emergency call from a woman with an overflowing drain. My father, grumbling a little about having to work on Sunday, departed with his bag to sort it.

For dinner we had sausages and mashed turnip.

'Couldn't afford a roast,' said my mother.

'I like sausages,' I said.

'A fine piece of roast pork and crackling's a good sight better,' said my father.

'I bet you didn't have roast meat every week when you were a boy,' I said.

'I'm not wanting to go back to those times. My parents were aye hard up, they had trouble to make ends meet. A forester wasn't very well paid in those days. We lived off porridge and broth many's a time.'

'Nothing wrong with that,' I said.

'Would you fancy it?'

'You've never liked porridge for a start,' said my mother.

It was really a funny conversation for we had had it before, backwards, with my father telling me how lucky I was and that I shouldn't automatically expect to be eating expensive food all the time and I'd be no worse off if I'd had his diet as a boy! He went back to the glen as seldom as possible; he had adopted Glasgow whole-heartedly and wanted nothing else.

I finished painting the bathroom in the afternoon, wrote out a new ad. for Tuesday evening's papers, stressing the twenty-four-hour service part, and also offering ten per cent off all commissions in the coming fortnight. About the latter I did not consult my father for I did not feel up to an argument. But we had to do something to get the business moving.

CHAPTER NINE

THE AD. in Tuesday evening's papers brought a number of enquiries. The phone rang fairly constantly between five and ten in the evening; I sat in the shop answering it. 'McKinley and Campbell, Plumbing Engineers. May I help you?' and felt terribly efficient. The more I answered the more secretarial did my voice become until I began to feel maybe I was going to miss my true calling after all.

There were two calls for my father and uncle to answer immediately. They went without enthusiasm, needless to say, for the jobs were not large.

'But I've said twenty-four-hour service,' I told them. 'For jobs large or small.'

'And you've promised ten per cent off too.' My father thumped the newspaper. 'Without consulting us.'

'But it's making folk ring.' Fortunately the phone rang again then, releasing me. After I'd said my bit, I heard an amused voice at the other end of the line.

'James!'

'James!' said my father, shaking his head.

'One moment please.' I was well into the patter now and doing it automatically. I covered the receiver with my hand. 'You'd better get on out to Bearsden, Dad. I promised the woman you'd be there in half-an-hour.'

He humphed, picked up his bag and left.

'It isn't easy running a business,' I told James. 'Trying to keep everybody happy. I'll ring you back later when things are quieter.'

In the course of the evening I got six enquiries for fairly big jobs, replumbing, installing new water tanks, new bathroom suites, things like that, and several minor ones. It gave me great satisfaction to note them all down in my book. I did not scrawl with my usual carelessness; I wrote meticulously the name, address and work to be estimated for. Then I drew up a schedule for my father and uncle for the next two days.

When they returned at ten, having taken a detour via the local pub, I gave each of them a work sheet.

'Isn't it great?' I said.

'But it's only estimates we're doing, it doesn't mean we'll get the work,' said my father.

'Oh, you're such a pessimist!' I cried with fury.

'At least it's a start, Andrew,' said Uncle Tam.

'But neither of us has ever done any estimating before.'

'You'll have to make them fairly low then,' I said.

'We can't make them too low or it won't be worth us going out. Especially with that ten per cent off and all.'

They went upstairs to get a cup of tea. I dialled James's number and got his mother.

'Oh yes, Maggie, how are you, dear?'

I said I was fine and we talked for a bit about the business, then I gathered courage to ask for James.

'He's in the middle of a long history essay, dear. I don't really think – '

'Okay.' I sighed. 'Would you tell him I called?'

She said goodnight, and the phone went dead. I had no confidence that she would tell him; she was a very honest woman, or liked to think she was anyway, and so she'd probably comfort herself by thinking she had forgotten.

History essays reminded me that I had geography homework to do. It was midnight before I crawled to bed but as it turned out I needn't have wasted my time doing it for I didn't get to school in the morning.

At five a.m. the phone rang. My mother called out to me to go and answer it. 'You and your twenty-four-hour service,' she said, as I staggered, half-blind, past her open bedroom door. My father was still snoring, in spite of the insistent shrill coming from the sitting room. He could sleep through a revolution.

It was Uncle Tam on the phone. Aunt Jessie was in agony, he said, doubled up with pain, and he was waiting for the doctor. Could my mother come over?

My mother was out of bed in a flash, moving faster than I'd ever seen her, shaking my father and taking her rollers out at the same time. I went to the kitchen and made them a cup of tea. My mother drank two cups whilst she combed her hair out and put on her coat.

'Hurry up, Andrew,' she called.

He came into the kitchen with his hair standing on end and his braces hanging. He looked bewildered. I put a cup of tea into his hand. I watched them drive away from the sitting room window, then I went back to bed for there was nothing else I could do for Aunt Jessie. I fell asleep again and woke to the sound of the phone ringing. It was now seven o'clock. I staggered, half-blind, to answer it.

My mother said that the doctor had called for an ambulance to take Aunt Jessie to hospital and that Aunt Jessie wanted her to go with her. The doctor thought it was appendicitis. My mother said that I had better stay off school and look after the shop, answer the phone and all that, my father would be home in a wee while and she'd be back sometime. And I was to see that Jean and Sandy got up and weren't late for school.

I went back to bed and fell asleep again, woke the next time at half-past eight, so that it was panic-stations all round with Jean moaning that they'd never make it and Sandy shouting at me as if it was all my fault. The phone rang in the middle of it and it was some silly woman gushing on about a washer for her hot tap until I had to say, 'Sorry, madam, but we have an emergency here. Could you call back later?' I thrust buttered rolls and school books into Jean and Sandy's arms, and threw them out.

'If you're late you can blame me,' I shouted after them. 'Everybody'll believe you.'

I was clearing up the chaos they had left in their wake when my father returned.

'Tam'll be no use for anything today. He was up half the night and he's worried sick. I'll just have to manage without him.'

It would have to happen on the very day they had work to do! For the few days before that they'd been sitting in the back shop playing cards to pass the time.

Around midday my mother phoned to say that Aunt Jessie had been operated on for appendicitis and everything had gone off all right. She herself was back with my Uncle Tam but thought she'd have to spend the day there giving him a hand. Their children were younger than us three and someone would have to cook their tea. It would not be Uncle Tam, who was as handless as my father in the kitchen. I was beginning to think there was something to be said for the Frasers' ways, for their men could cook almost as well as their women.

'Everything all right there?' asked my mother.

'Fine. Dad's out, I'm in. McKinley and Campbell are flourishing.'

Not true exactly, but we were not static any longer. My father had looked in mid-morning and said one job was a dead duck at least: the woman obviously did not have two brass farthings to rub together and thought you could replumb a house for about a hundred pounds. It would be a waste of paper writing out her estimate, but write it I did, in my newly acquired elegant hand. Mr Scott would never believe it if I was to give in an essay as well written as that. Thinking of Mr Scott made me uneasy for I should have had an English class that morning. So it was no surprise when he dropped in to the shop on the way home. The trouble was he lived too close to me now, and could easily find out what I was up to.

'It had better be a good story, Maggie!'

It was, and he could say nothing against it. How could I have abandoned my family in their hour of need?

'Your family always seems to be in need.'

'Aunt Jessie couldn't help her appendix bursting.'

'No, indeed.' He sighed. He sat in one of the armchairs and unbuttoned his coat.

'Would you like a cup of coffee?'

'I wouldn't mind.' He had had a tiring day: three first year classes and a difficult second year apart from my own class. 'Some of them haven't an original thought in their heads. At least you do, Maggie. That's why it would annoy me so much if you let things slide.'

I was not letting things slide, I protested, I was a victim of circumstances. He said that he thought he should have a talk with my parents, who did not seem to appreciate how much work I had to do to take my Highers next May. Not just now, I pleaded, please, for they had enough on their plates as it was. You see, it was not that they wanted to hold me back, but because I was sixteen and *could* have left school they didn't think it mattered too much if I had the odd day or two off. They were more fussy about Jean and Sandy not being off, even though both of them intended to leave the first chance they got and give up studying for ever.

'I'll make it,' I said.

'Well, I hope so.' Mr Scott stood up, buttoned his coat. 'Thanks for the coffee. By the way, can you manage to baby-sit tonight?'

'Yes, I've got Jean lined up to answer the phone here.'

If I didn't want to then it didn't matter, he said, but I wanted to go for I needed the money. Since I had given up my Saturday job I had had much less to manage on and I couldn't expect my father to pay me anything when we weren't even covering our overheads. He moaned every meal-time about how his savings were disappearing like snow off a dyke.

I took my books with me to the Scotts and enjoyed

the peace and quiet. I hadn't realised before how irritating the sound of the frequent ringing of the phone could be. When I had done a certain amount of work I allowed myself the luxury of ringing James. It was a treat I had been looking forward to all day. His mother answered again. She must have been sitting beside the phone every evening just in case I rang, probably doing her macramé so that she wouldn't waste her time.

'Oh, James is out, dear.'

Out! Jealousy surged in me like hot bile. It was ridiculous of me to feel like that for he was probably not doing anything for me to be jealous about, but I had imagined him glued to his work every night, suffering, and certainly not enjoying himself. Would he be in later? I tried not to sound too bothered. She did not know when he would be back, and she was not going to tell me where he was either; she was going to let me writhe in agony and uncertainty. When I had rung off I sat and stared into the fire imagining him at a party or dancing with some girl at a disco. Crazy fool McKinley! Could you see him doing that? The trouble was that right then I was in such a frazzled state of mind that I could.

He rang the next evening. I was cool.

'Oh yes, hello.'

'Are you all right, Maggie?'

'What do you mean – am I all right? I'm just fine. Fine.' I hoped I sounded not only fine, but bored, with him.

'What's been doing with you?'

'Nothing much.' That was a lie for we had had another hectic day of my mother visiting Aunt Jessie at

104

hospital, feeding Aunt Jessie's kids, and me taking the morning off school yet again.

We had a moment's silence, then he asked, 'Is there anything wrong?'

Then he got it, full blast. I had been all pent up, one way and another, and James was a suitable target to let fly at. I informed him that I had phoned him twice in a row and he hadn't even phoned back (I gave him no chance to butt in and offer excuses, though I could hear him trying to), and last night, after I'd had the most terrible day with Aunt Jessie being rushed to hospital and dear knows what else, he had been out gallivanting, probably with some other female, when I'd wanted to talk to him.

'Would you shut up?' he shouted at length down the phone, which quite surprised me as he had never raised his voice to me before. I did shut up. He had not known I had phoned yesterday evening, and he had been gallivanting at the school debating society of which he was president.

I had known, deep inside me, that there would be some explanation like that, but for some reason or other I had needed that outburst. There are times when I feel driven to extremes and say all kinds of mad things and know, even when I'm saying them, that they're mad.

Meekly, I said to James that I was sorry.

'That's all right. I know you're under a strain, Maggie. Look here, I'm coming through to see you on Saturday, yes I am, just for the day.'

What would his mother say? Plenty no doubt. But he was old enough to do what he wanted, he said, and if she didn't like it that was too bad. It would certainly not make me any more popular with her, but I couldn't help that, and I wanted to see him too much to stop him.

'Tell me, Maggie,' he said, 'did you feel jealous at the thought that I might be out with some other female?'

'Jealous? Why should I feel jealous?'

He chuckled. He was delighted that I had been jealous, and my face burned, making me glad that I was unseen by him. There had been a time when I wouldn't even let him know that I liked him. I had never fancied the idea of getting too dependent on somebody and here I was all worked up because I hadn't set eyes on him for not quite two weeks! I was not altogether pleased with myself. Perhaps his mother had a point or two in what she'd said. I went round to talk to Janet Scott about it.

'Well, you are young to get too involved, Maggie. Especially with your plans for a career ahead. Although of course there's no reason why a woman can't have marriage and a career these days. Though children do complicate things. You can see that with me.'

'Marriage! Children!' I was horrified, didn't want to think about things like that as if they could affect *me*. I decided that I would cease to think about James and me, let things be. When something is too disturbing and I don't know what to do I push it out of the way and become ostrich-like. I had more pressing affairs to cope with, anyway.

We got one definite commission for the installation of a new bathroom suite from a woman in Hillhead, which improved my father's spirits, and we had several small immediate jobs which brought in a little bit. I was doing a big trade in hardware equipment for there was no other shop selling the stuff for a mile, so I stocked up on that and had a great time raking round the warehouses. Jean and Lorraine were sewing like mad, which meant that they were neglecting their homework, and this led me to get another little lecture from Mr Scott. He seemed to drop into the shop almost every afternoon on his way home from school, and usually it was not to offer praises. One or two women in the district said they would like to sew and knit articles that I could sell, so I accepted on condition that we took a certain percentage in commission. 'What next, Maggie McKinley?' my mother asked daily. 'I'm not sure sometimes what kind of shop we're supposed to be running.'

Did it matter? I was building up the McKinley empire. Some empire! We were still eating sausages and beans on toast, for apart from us five McKinleys there were quite a number of Campbell mouths to feed. It might have been a shade off empire-building but it was turning out to be a full-time job, what with Aunt Jessie unable to help and my mother only there half the time; and around it I had to fit in school. I was glad when Friday came.

I was even more glad when Saturday came.

I was a quarter of an hour early for James's train and I had to walk up and down the cold station to keep myself warm. It seemed like years since I had waited for him here before. I eyed the magazines on the stand but had no money to waste. I had hardly any money in my pocket at all these days, a strange state of affairs for Maggie McKinley to be in for I had always managed to be earning something from my earliest years. When I was a wee kid I had 'run messages' for the neighbours, who had rewarded me with enough to keep me in sweets and crisps.

I was on the platform when the train came chugging in. I saw a door flying open before the engine came to rest, knew it would be James and began to run. We almost knocked one another over and his chin struck my eye, which left a lovely bruise later but at the time was not felt.

'Maggie, I've missed you! Why can't you live in Edinburgh?'

'Why can't you live in Glasgow?'

We hugged one another and laughed and he gave me a birl. My feet narrowly missed a passing porter, who seemed less entranced with the world than we were that wet, cold, Saturday morning in Glasgow. Outside it was dark November at its nastiest but, in spite of the wind and the rain, we walked all the way home so that we would be on our own for as long as possible. I was strongly tempted not to go back. I said so.

'Let's run away,' said James.

'Where to?'

'The glen?'

'Yes. Or Greenyards. That would be even further.'

'You want to return to your origins?' he said teasingly.

'Maybe. Go back to where my great-great-granny came from, find an old ruined croft and build it up again.'

'And live happily ever after!' He smiled at me and

squeezed my hand. His mother was right: we were getting too intense, even with the rain bashing down at a rate that would have dampened most normal people's ardour. Perhaps it was as well that the shop and my family were waiting for us.

My mother and father were easier with James now and greeted him warmly, for them. My mother fussed over his wet clothes and hung them on the pulley, leaving me to get rid of my own, then she made him tea, scrambled egg and toast, which she kindly allowed me to share. She sat at the table with us whilst we ate and told James the tale of Aunt Jessie's appendectomy. She appeared to think he would understand the mechanics of it since he had intentions of becoming a doctor.

'But of course you'll ken all about it, James,' she said.

'Mum, he hasn't started yet. He's still at school.'

She paid no attention to me, she had her eyes fixed on James. They had such a good thing going between them that I left them alone and went down to open up the shop. I sold five toilet rolls, a packet of dustbin liners, two plastic basins and a cloth dog before he appeared.

We had a busy morning, though not everyone who came in bought anything, for we had my Campbell cousins, Jean and Lorraine, my friend Isobel, who had heard James was coming and wanted to check him over, and the Scotts, who were passing. I made a lot of instant coffee.

'It's like a social club, this place,' said Janet.

In the afternoon things were quieter and most of the time James and I were on our own.

Just after two I had a telephone call from a distraught female. Her sink was blocked, her drain was blocked and overflowing, she had six weans and couldn't get their nappies washed (I could hear some of them wailing in the background), and her husband was away at the football. . . . I cut off her saga of domestic woe and said, 'Leave it to me.' Leave it to me! That was all very well but my father and uncle were away at the football too, even though the rain was still bucketing down, and I was well aware that their idea of giving twenty-four-hour service did not cover Saturday afternoons. Football time was sacred, and if all the drains in Glasgow were blocked they'd have to stay that way till the final whistle blew.

The phone rang, and it was the woman again. I had said someone was coming, hadn't I? We did offer twenty-four-hour service, didn't we? Yes, yes, I told her, we had the matter in hand. I turned to James. What were we to do? We didn't want to let down our reputation. Certainly not before we had built one up.

'I'll go,' said James.

'You?'

'Why not? I'm sure I can unblock a drain and a sink. You don't think we send for a plumber every time we have a blocked sink in our house, do you?'

No, now that I came to think of it, I could not imagine it, not with his mother running the show. 'But you don't look like a plumber,' I objected.

'Do I have to? And what on earth does a plumber look like?'

'But in those trousers and that corduroy jacket – '

'I could borrow a pair of your father's overalls, couldn't I? I don't suppose he would mind.'

Whether he would mind or not was of no importance. Since he was not here to do the job he would have no say in the matter.

I found a pair of overalls and James put them on. He was a few inches taller than my father and so the trousers came half way up his legs, making him look very funny. I laughed until my stomach ached.

'Well, I'm glad I amuse you so much, but I think I'll have to do. Can we take your father's van?'

'We're going to.' He wouldn't like that either, James driving his van, but there was a good chance we would get back before he did. He had gone to the match in Uncle Tam's car. I got Jean to tend the shop and accompanied James.

The woman's house was chaotic, ten times worse than the Scotts' ever was, which I had not thought possible. Wet nappies and other assorted baby clothes hung steaming from every projection in the kitchen and sitting room. She had had twins a month before, she told me, so I commiserated and listened to her tale of sleepless nights and vomiting babies. It turned out that she only had two other children, not four. I had felt, listening to her on the phone that it must be six in all. I told her to relax, our plumber would soon have the whole mess sorted. We followed James into the kitchen and she removed from the sink a basin of soaking nappies that smelt unbelievably bad, a pile of dirty crockery from the draining board, and from the floor, a toy train on which James had almost broken his neck. Upstairs the babies were yowling but she did not go to them, remaining where she was, arms folded, to watch the operation.

James looked fantastically efficient. He got plungers

and things out of my father's tool bag and within minutes the dirty water was gurgling away down the drain, which was of course blocked outside. We accompanied James to the doorway and watched the second part from the shelter of the porch. He looked as if he was enjoying himself and when he knelt down to the drain he gave me a big wink. I wondered what Mrs Fraser would think if he changed his mind suddenly and decided to go into the plumbing business. He could join McKinley and Campbell, that well-known firm of Glasgow plumbing engineers!

He stood up. 'That's it free now.'

The woman was tremendously grateful and offered us tea, cakes, coffee, biscuits, but nothing would have persuaded me to eat or drink in that house. I was more interested in being offered payment – we had looked up what the fee should be beforehand – but she did pay up without murmuring and said that if she ever needed a plumber again she would have none but James. James smiled sweetly upon her and we shut the door on the sound of squalling children.

'What a scene!' I shuddered. 'All those babies and nappies are not for me.'

'It doesn't have to be like that.'

'No? I'd rather not take the risk. I might end up no better able to cope than she is.'

'I would doubt that,' said James.

Our return coincided neatly with that of my father's. Uncle Tam's car turned in at one end of the street as we turned in at the other.

My father was a bit put out by the idea that James had been able to do his job, but he took it quite well and even said thank you, gruffly, but audibly. 'There's nothing much to clearing a drain of course,' he said.

He was right in that, for I had watched James carefully, and two nights later, when we got a call through at midnight from another distraught woman (why do they all ring us?), I decided against wakening my father and answered the call myself since she only lived walking distance away.

'Are you the plumber?' she asked when she opened the door to me. She eyed me with great suspicion, as if I might be a con-woman.

'I am.' I held up my bag to prove it. 'Women's lib has come a long way.'

'I thought it would be Mr McKinley that would come. He came before. Lovely man that.'

I stared at her, unbelievingly. My father a lovely man? This elderly woman with a cardigan pinned across her chest seemed to think so. Well!

She was lonely, that I realised after a couple of minutes, and that was why she had called out a plumber at that hour of night.

'You do offer twenty-four-hour service, don't you?' she said, looking guilty now.

'Yes.'

'Even for small jobs like this?'

'Yes.'

I fiddled about with the plunger and undid the trap on the pipe under the sink. It took me ten minutes to get it clear.

'You're awful clever.'

'Not really.'

'But for a lassie!'

I delivered her a little lecture on the capabilities of women, based on a two-minute talk I had once given in school. She looked very impressed, though I could sense she was not really interested. She offered me a cup of tea, which I accepted, for I could see the loneliness concealed in her eyes, and I was not all that tired. My plumbing expertise had exhilarated me and put me in no mood for sleep. I stayed half-an-hour and told her 'How to Succeed in Plumbing'. She said I was a real comic and I should try to get on the telly. There was a danger my head might swell to alarming proportions that night.

Walking home with my fee in my pocket I decided that I was going to be selfish and spend it on a new sweater. I reckoned I deserved it.

CHAPTER TEN

I BROUGHT up the question of my going to Inverness-shire for New Year with my mother when she was in a good mood. Aunt Jessie had been discharged from hospital and the firm had landed a fairly big job which would keep my father and uncle busy for a couple of weeks at least; but as soon as I mentioned going away at Hogmanay my mother's face changed.

'But, Maggie, you ken fine I like having you all round me for the New Year.'

'I know, Mum, but just this once – '

'There might not be many more years that we'll be together. You'll get married – '

'I won't. Not for years.'

'You'll be away at the university, then.'

'But I'll come home for holidays. Anyway, I might go to Glasgow University.' This I had little intention of doing, for I considered that by then it would be time for me to spread my wings a bit wider.

'Maggie, it wouldne be the same if you weren't here.'

I sighed, and gave up. She was getting agitated. There was no point in arguing further, or trying to persuade her, and I should have known it before I started, for New Year is the most important time of the year to my mother and she follows all the old Scots' customs of cleaning her house on Old Year's night, not allowing anyone fair to first-foot her, and she provides the traditional fare of shortbread and black bun whilst my father provides the drink. She expects to see all her family over the New Year period so that they can eat and drink together. She would have let me go for Christmas, for that was less important to her. I supposed that with the Frasers it would be the other way round: they are more anglicised. When I told James that, he didn't like it; he said he was Scots to the bone, had not an ounce of English blood in him. It is the old class thing again, I suppose. The social customs of the Edinburgh middle and upper-middle classes! Contrast with the social customs of the Glasgow lower-middle and working classes. Good topic for an essay. I suggested it to Mr Scott, who dismissed it scornfully. He said I was the only one in the class interested in the subject.

James was very fed up when he heard that I would not be able to come to the glen with them.

'But, Maggie, surely – '

'There's no surely about it. My mother won't change her mind because she can't. It's not a case of being mean.'

'No, I know.' He sighed. 'Well, I won't go either then. I'll come to Glasgow for the week instead.'

'That'll upset your mother.'

It certainly did, and the next time I rang and she answered the phone, she told me so quite definitely.

'You're staying at home to be with your mother, Maggie, so how do you think I'm going to feel about James being away?'

'I didn't ask him not to go, Mrs Fraser,' I said very coolly, just holding my anger in check. I was getting a bit fed up with her laying everything at my door. Did she think her son was such a weakling that everything he did was because I told him to and not because he wanted to? If she didn't lay off I was going to ask her that question.

'But couldn't you ask your mother to do without you just this once?'

I explained to Mrs Fraser my mother's feeling concerning New Year. 'It's just the way you feel about having James and Catriona for Christmas.'

She was quiet for a moment, then she said, 'I tell you what, Maggie, why don't you come through for Christmas? Come for two or three days.' And then James could spend the New Year with them. She did not add that, did not need to, but I got the message loud and clear and knew that I was being offered two or three days in Edinburgh to buy me off spending New Year with James. 'We'd love to have you, dear, and if you say your mother doesn't mind about Christmas. . . .'

I would think about it, I said, and let her know. And think about it I did, even during the night when I would have been better off sleeping. There was no point in making a total enemy out of Mrs Fraser: it would do none of us any good. I liked her a lot of the time and if it hadn't been for James we'd have got on very well together. My mother, when I broached it with her, said that I could go for Christmas if I wanted to, she didn't mind. So I rang Mrs Fraser back and accepted and I told James that he should go with his

117

family up to Inverness-shire for New Year.

'Okay, I suppose I should.' He sounded weary of the topic, no doubt he had been subjected to a steady attack and was ready to settle for a bit of peace. 'Catriona says now that she's not going unless Alexander is invited.'

Mrs Fraser might have had her problems, but we were not lacking any either. Work was coming in in a steady trickle but several customers were slow or loath to pay their bills.

'It's always the way in business,' said Aunt Jessie, who was back in the shop to do her stint. She was looking fine, had had her hair newly permed and dyed red. 'Folk and their money are no easy parted.'

I took it upon myself to visit one or two of them in person, those whose accounts were largest, and told them a long tale of starving kids and crushing overheads. They did in fact cough up, saying that it had just kept slipping their minds, they had meant to pay, etc. Debt collector McKinley! What would I be doing next? I preferred not to think.

The weeks leading up to Christmas moved fast and furiously. Many people made things for us to sell and almost as soon as we displayed them we disposed of them. I bought in cards, wrapping paper, tinsel, and tree decorations, and Janet Scott said it was great to be able to buy all these things so close at hand.

We had a couple of cold snaps and a number of burst pipes. It was seldom that my father and uncle found time to play cards in the back shop, and my father was even able to grumble about being run off his feet. I worked hard at school and at home in the evenings, going to bed dead beat every night at twelve. The twenty-four-hour service business I coped with by taking the receiver off the hook on the nights we were all too tired to move. James said that was cheating (he was only teasing) and I said that there were times when one had to cheat to stay alive. Most people who rang for a plumber at three in the morning could well wait till seven.

James I did not see from that Saturday when he had played plumber until Christmas Eve. We had agreed that we would wait out that period, since we both had a great deal to do and also so that we would not annoy our families too much. But we phoned regularly and wrote letters. I liked to get a letter from him for then I could carry it around all day and read it many times. On one occasion, when I was reading an epistle from James instead of listening to Mr Scott, I had it confiscated, all ten pages. Mr Scott returned it to me at the end of the lesson, after I had meekly apologised.

'Of course I know I can't hope to compete with James for your attention, so perhaps you'd better not bring his letters into my class another time.'

I said that I would not. I folded up the letter and stuffed it in my pocket.

'I never thought I'd see the day, Maggie, when you of all people would be so love-sick!'

'Love-sick! Me? Rubbish!'

My father gave me some money to buy presents – he said I had earned it and I felt good, for to give praise doesn't come easily to him – and I went down town to shop one Saturday. Glasgow was looking great, decorated and strung with masses of lights (we do things like that well in Glasgow) and the shops were full of incredible things that made my eyes bulge. It was a long time since I had wandered around the town, in and out of the shops, gloating over well-stocked counters. I love shops, even when they're busy and people rush you in all directions.

The school term ended and I went to a couple of parties, one of them at the Scotts who invited a mixture of people of differing ages. I enjoyed myself.

'You should go out more often, Maggie,' said Janet. 'You can't sit at home waiting for James all the time. Not at your age!'

'Don't you start!' I told her, for I often heard the same thing at home. Aunt Jessie was the only one who said, 'Never you mind, hen, a good man's worth waiting for, and there aren't too many of them around, I can tell you!'

In the end, Christmas Eve came, although there had been moments when I thought it never would or that I would wake up one morning and find I'd missed it. My family and I exchanged our presents, all of us getting just what we wanted, having dropped large hints to one another beforehand, and I set off for Edinburgh.

James was there, waiting for me. It was late afternoon and the lights were lit in Princes Street, and above all floated the flood-lit castle looking like something out of a fairy tale. The Frasers, who all seemed happy and at ease with each other, were gathered in their upstairs drawing room which shimmered with tinsel and coloured baubles, and glowed with warmth and light from a big log fire. There was a smell of wood-smoke and tangerines.

'Nice to see you, Maggie,' said Mr Fraser, getting up at once.

'Very nice,' said Grandfather, also rising to make me feel like an honoured guest.

'Yes, we're glad you could come, dear,' said Mrs Fraser, offering me her flushed cheek. In her kitchen downstairs I saw how busy she had been: the shelves were stacked with tins of Christmas cake, mince pies, shortbread, chocolate cake, orange cake, home-made sweets, and in the larder sat an enormous turkey already stuffed.

We had a lovely evening, eating, drinking, talking, relaxing in front of the sweet-smelling fire, and outside the wind raged, making us feel even cosier. Mrs Fraser suggested Scrabble – even on Christmas Eve she seemed to feel a need to be doing something – but no one was interested so she fetched her macramé and her fingers worked away busily at that.

'You should take a rest, Elizabeth,' said Grandfather.

'But I am resting,' she said in surprise.

'Elizabeth can't sit with her hands doing nothing, you know that, Father,' said Mr Fraser.

'Just as well,' she said, but without tartness, 'otherwise nothing would get done around here.'

At midnight she wound up her ball of string and declared that it was time for bed. Grandfather was dozing quietly in his armchair already. James and I managed to linger on in the drawing room whilst she tidied up and everyone dispersed.

'Stay a minute,' he murmured.

We were sitting on the settee together. He put his arm round me and I let my head lie on his shoulder.

He told me that I was looking very pretty in my new dress. It was a long dress, of green velvet, that Jean had made for me, and in it I felt very composed, serene almost, you might say. Serene, you, Maggie McKinley! I could imagine my mother's voice.

At the neck of the dress I was wearing a Cairngorm brooch, given to me by my granny. It had belonged to her and her granny before her. From time to time I touched it, and when I did I thought of both women, one whom I knew well in the flesh, the other in my imagination. Touching the brooch pleased me, and made me feel peaceful deep down inside me.

The door opened quietly behind us, and we heard James's mother's voice, in the flesh, 'Come on then, you two, you'll never get up in the morning for your presents if you don't get to bed!' She sounded bright and cheery, when underneath you knew she must have been feeling irritated and apprehensive. James started to protest that we were not five years old, but she ignored that and began to rake out the ashes of the fire and sweep up the grate. We were obliged to go to bed.

In the morning, after present-giving, James and I went out for a walk. The wind had calmed in the night and the sun was shining. I felt slightly guilty that I had not offered to help his mother but James said that she did not need help, although she often asked for it because she couldn't bear to see anyone idle.

'But she means well,' he said.

'Oh yes, I know.'

She was what my granny would call a 'good woman'. Thinking of my granny brought a lump to my throat and I wondered what she was doing this

Christmas morning. I had sent her a pair of woolly bedsocks, a mohair scarf (in sludge green so that there was a chance she would wear it), and a photograph of Sandy, Jean and me to put on her mantelpiece. She would point it out proudly to all her callers. She loved family photographs, even though she didn't see very much of her family. My mother had written to invite her to come down to Glasgow for New Year, knowing full well that she would never come. She had never once set foot in the dirty city and never would now.

'You'll go and see my granny when you're up north?' I asked James.

'Of course. I'll go as often as I can.'

'She'll be pleased.'

'More pleased if you were to come.'

I shrugged. What could I do? It was my mother or my granny, and even my granny would have no difficulty in deciding who should come first.

Christmas dinner was delicious and engorging, and afterwards James, Catriona and I took a few staggers through Queen Street Gardens to try to work off the effects of our excess eating. Alexander had gone home to his family in Fife for the holiday so Catriona had not seen him and was inclined to be mournful.

In bed that night she confided to me that she had invited Alexander up to the glen for New Year. 'He's coming up on the train the day after us.'

'But, Catriona, what will your mother say?'

'What can she say if he just arrives?'

'But does *he* know?'

Of course he did not. It promised to be an explosive week but Catriona refused to be deterred, she said it would be all right once he was there for they could go out together for long walks up the glen and her mother would get a chance to know Alexander and would probably end up by liking him.

'You see, Maggie, she won't even give him a chance.'

On Boxing Night the Frasers gave a party for about thirty people. Some were friends of the Mr and Mrs and Grandfather, and some were friends of James and Catriona. Catriona and I helped Mrs Fraser prepare sandwiches and savouries, and James and his father made hot punch. We had a tremendous evening and I liked everybody I met. One or two of James's school friends said, 'Ah, so you're James's Maggie!' and I felt proud and pleased. We danced to music on the record player and I noticed that even Mrs Fraser was up on the floor several times, laughing, her cheeks pink and smiling.

The morning after was less cheery, as mornings after tend to be. James and I had to say goodbye again.

'I hate goodbyes,' I said, as we stood in the station clutching one another.

'Let's not say the word any more,' suggested James and when the time came to part he said, 'See you soon, Maggie. Look after yourself, and a Happy New Year when it comes!'

I, who seldom give way to tears, have to admit to a certain moisture in my eyes as the train puffed through Princes Street Gardens and entered the long black tunnel at the end of it.

It was tea-time when I reached home. The shop was dark but the lights were on in the flat. My parents were alone in the sitting room.

'What's the matter?' I asked as soon as I saw their faces.

'It's your granny,' said my mother.

'*What*?'

'Take it easy, love, she's just ill, that's all.'

I subsided a little. For one moment I had thought – Well, she was eighty-three after all and it was ridiculous to think she could live forever. But it was bad enough that she was ill.

'We had a letter from her neighbour,' said my father, handing it to me.

Mrs Clark said that Granny had been ill with 'flu for several days and was making heavy weather of it but absolutely refused to go to hospital, saying that if she was going to die she was going to do it in her own house. Cussed old thing that she was! Mrs Clark was worried about her and didn't know what to do.

'Somebody'll need to go,' said my mother.

Both she and my father looked at me, but I did not have to be drafted.

CHAPTER ELEVEN

MY DRIVE north with the Frasers was a mixture of pleasure at being with James after all and of apprehension as to how I should find my granny. Mrs Fraser sensibly said that I should not worry, there was nothing I could do until I got there and I was well on my way, so I might as well relax and enjoy the journey. She was very kind to me and I knew I could rely on her help with Granny if I needed it. Her strength calmed me.

The countryside, in its bare winter beauty, also calmed me. The trees stood stark and black against the hills and the blue, pink and mauve-tinged sky. The further north we went and the later in the day it became the more colours appeared in the sky. Yellow, orange, red, purplish-grey, shades of blue, green and even black. . . . It was incredible.

'Winter skies are always the loveliest,' said Mr Fraser.

There was snow lying on the tops of the hills and in north-facing crevices. It was early yet for skiing, though one or two cars did pass us with skis on the roof.

'I'm going to take you up on the hill behind the cottage,' said James. 'Yes, I am! You'll love it, with the crisp snow on top, and the air's fantastically clear at

126

this time of year.' He held my hand all the way, which also helped to calm me.

The blue in the sky deepened, and in the west a broad band of sizzling orange-pink streaked the horizon. Within a short time it had gone, leaving the sky to become blue-black sprinkled with fine winking stars.

'I don't know why we have to live in the city,' said Mr Fraser, echoing my thoughts.

We pulled up at my granny's door. The light was on in her bedroom behind the drawn curtain. I sprang out of the car, closely followed by James and then his mother. Before I had time to ring the bell or try the door Mrs Clark appeared at the top of the stairs.

'Is it you, Maggie?'

'Yes. Is she all right?'

'Just the same. Hang on a minute and I'll let you in. I have a key.'

She went into her own flat, came back with it. Her hair was blued as before, and she was looking fresh and chirpy. 'She's lying there, not much caring about anything.'

It did not sound at all like my granny. Mrs Clark opened the door and we filed in.

'It's me, Mrs McKinley,' called out Mrs Clark, going to the bedroom door. 'And guess who I've got with me? A late Christmas present for you!'

I put my head round the door and saw my granny lying on her back in bed with her hands folded on the coverlet.

'Maggie!' She looked as if she could not believe it. 'Is it you, lass?'

'It is, Gran.' I went up to the bed. 'I've come to spend the New Year with you.' I leant over and kissed her old worn cheek. She grasped my hand tightly in hers but said nothing more. She looked exhausted and feverish.

Mrs Fraser took charge. She dismissed Mrs Clark, in the nicest possible way, for Mrs Clark was inclined to prattle, which would exhaust a well person let alone a sick one, then she sent James and his father for the doctor so that we could find out what we should be doing for Granny. The doctor, whom we all knew, came very soon and said that Granny should be kept warm, given lots of liquid to drink regularly, some good beef broth if possible, and that she must take her medicine, which she usually forgot to do if she was not bullied.

'Will she be all right, doctor?' I asked anxiously. We were in the sitting room with the door closed to her bedroom.

'Difficult to say, Maggie. Probably. But she's a good age, don't forget!'

Mrs Fraser sent her husband, James and Catriona off to their cottage; she stayed with me and we spent the night in sleeping bags on the sitting-room floor. We left Granny's door open and several times during the night when we heard her stir or moan we jumped up and gave her a drink and sponged off her forehead. At times she did not seem to know who I was, at others she would grip my hand and say my name over and over again.

In the morning she lay sleeping, breathing peacefully, the fevered look gone. When the doctor came we sat her up and she found her tongue which reassured me. 'What a fuss to be making about a wee drop 'flu,' she said.

'We need to make a fuss,' said the doctor, 'or you wouldn't pay the slightest bit of attention.'

When he had examined her he said that her chest seemed much easier, her temperature was down and he thought that, with a bit of luck, she had passed the worst.

'I think maybe you were the right medicine for her, Maggie. Better than anything I could have prescribed.'

'I'm no sorry to see the lassie, I must admit,' said my granny. 'Though I must admit there's times she can be fair trying.'

'Now, Granny!' said I. 'Any more of your nonsense and I'll be away back to Glasgow.'

'What would anybody want to go to a place like that for?'

The doctor said that she should stay in bed until he returned and no nonsense about getting up even for a wee while. I said that I would see to it that she obeyed orders. I would bully her all that was necessary.

'I've no doubt,' said my granny with a sigh, but there was a wee hint of a smile upon her lips too.

She took some breakfast since it was prepared and brought to her bedside by Mrs Fraser, whom she would not like to refuse.

'Now then, Mrs McKinley, eat up your scrambled egg, every little bit! It'll do you good.'

It was an effort for Granny to eat it but she did, then she lay back on the pillows. Even that had tired her and she seemed very weak.

'Sleep now,' said Mrs Fraser. 'Maggie and I will be in the next room.'

The rest of the Frasers arrived and were relieved to hear that Granny's condition had improved. James, who had been unable to sleep for worrying about her, had got up at six to walk to the head of the glen. I was glad I had not been there to be dragged along with him. I shivered at the thought of going up to the head of the glen at such an hour, when the air would be chill and the ground as hard as iron. The Frasers were as tough as my granny's old boots, even Catriona, for they had been reared to face the mountain tops in all weathers. It was still a mystery to me how I fitted in with them at all.

James, Catriona and I went shopping whilst Mr and Mrs Fraser stayed to keep an eye on Granny. All the shopkeepers remembered us and were pleased to see us again. It took a fair time to work our way along the village street (it is, in fact, considered to be a small town but nobody could take that seriously), by the time we chatted to this one and that one, and caught up with all the news on both sides. They wanted to know first of all how my granny was: they were anxious for her. The district nurse stopped in her car when she saw us and wound down the window.

'Nice to see you, Maggie. Have you come to look after your granny? I'm just away to see to her now. You'll do her the world of good, I'm sure.'

'Everyone expects me to work like a magician,' I said.

James smiled at me, squeezed my hand. 'You do at times.'

I looked at Catriona, suddenly remembering Alexander. 'What time does Alexander arrive?'

Her face went a bit pasty at the mention of his name. She swallowed and said, 'Two o'clock. Honestly, Maggie, I'm scared stiff now. What'll Mother say?'

Catriona's guess was as good as mine; better. She said that she felt sick (she looked it) and hoped that Alexander had managed to miss the train or had fallen ill, not seriously, but enough to prevent him travelling. It was a crazy idea, now that she was faced with it becoming reality, and she had thought it up in a mood of couldn't-care-less brought about by her mother's total refusal to even consider Alexander as a guest. We knew all that of course but Catriona had to spell it out for us, at the end of which she could blame none other than her mother, and this brought back her anger and dampened her sickness. A touch of pink appeared high on each cheek.

'She'll just have to put up with it.' Catriona tossed her head. 'I don't care.' I could not say she was totally convincing.

When we arrived back Mrs Fraser said, 'Where on earth have you been? You've taken ages. There is only one street in the village after all.' She did not expect an answer so she did not get one. 'Now then, Maggie, do you think you can manage without me? Your granny seems much better and the district nurse said she'd be in and out. I thought we'd all get back to the glen now and get things sorted.'

'Of course,' I said. 'You've been great. I don't know how I'd have – ' She cut short my thanks by saying that she'd done nothing and that if I needed her I'd only to

131

call. How I did not know, since they were not on the phone at the cottage. It would take a loud halloo to reach six miles, even in this clear air.

'I'll stay with Maggie for the day,' said James.

'I'll stay too,' said Catriona.

Their mother did not look one bit pleased, which made me feel guilty, for she had been so decent to my granny and me that I felt I ought to reward her by sending her family home with her. But Catriona's wish to stay had nothing to do with me, although her mother did not know it, and I was not going to force James to leave me, even if I could.

'Come on, Elizabeth,' said Mr Fraser. 'Let's leave the young ones to their own devices.'

He took her arm determinedly and led her out to the car.

'We'll come back later,' she called, 'and collect you.'

'Not before evening,' answered James.

'Don't tire Granny, all of you!' she admonished us, and then she was driven away.

'You don't think Alexander could stay here with you, do you?' said Catriona.

'What? In this wee house? I have to sleep on the sitting room floor as it is. I don't want Alexander for company, thank you very much!'

Catriona sighed. 'No, I didn't think you would.'

'You are an ass, Catriona,' said James, quite without sympathy.

Catriona declared that nobody cared about her troubles and she was going for a walk. She went. James and I stood for a moment in front of Granny's house looking towards the hills. They were completely white, outlined clearly against a very blue sky. The Frasers' cottage was set beneath those hills, as had been my granny's cottage before it was burnt.

Granny slept till lunch-time. I made some broth, not a patch on hers but edible, mince and potatoes, and rice pudding. All good sound fare that Granny would approve of, though when it came to eating it she disposed of only a little. The rest James and I dealt with, helped out by an old man who lived in the flat next door. Mr Farquharson came to the door just as I was serving the soup. He had come to enquire after Granny, he said.

His nose twitched. 'Fine smell, lassie. Is it broth you have in the pot?'

He was easily persuaded to sit at the kitchen table and take a bowl. He had a habit of calling at meal-times, when I was there at least. Some of his senses might be failing but smell was not amongst them.

Catriona did not come before two. I kept watching the clock. James said he was unconcerned about what she was up to; he had enough problems in his own life to sort out. I did not ask what they were.

'I hope she goes to meet him,' I said. 'He might be standing on the station platform, not knowing where to go. And freezing.'

A few minutes later James called to me from the window. 'Here they come!'

I joined him and saw Catriona coming up the path with Alexander who was decked out in a winter ski outfit, carrying a rucksack and skis. They looked as if they didn't know what to say to one another.

I opened the front door to them. 'Hi, Alexander!

133

Come on in.' I felt really sorry for him, as well as Catriona.

I made them coffee and found some shortbread in a tin. It was as hard as agate and about the same colour: part of Granny's New Year and Christmas baking. Her eyes were failing and half the time she couldn't tell if a thing was cooked or not. She usually trusted to luck, as good a way as any other, I often think.

We had a funny sort of afternoon. I had to spend a good part of it in Granny's room, though I did not stay too long at a stretch, and the rest of the time I tried to keep conversation going in the sitting room. Catriona sat by the fire, scorching her jeans and looking miserable; Alexander looked like a rabbit ready to run at the crack of a gun; and James looked fed up with both of them.

The day dwindled early and soon the hills could no longer be seen. It was pitch black outside and very quiet.

The Frasers came back at six, and it was a relief. We had been sitting there, waiting for the showdown for almost four hours.

Mrs Fraser was struck absolutely silent when she saw Alexander; her eyes bulged, her mouth opened, but her tongue refused to function. It was the first time I had ever seen her thus afflicted. I filled the gap. I talked about Granny, and Mr Farquharson, and Mrs Clark, and the district nurse, and anything else I could think of, and by the time I had run down, Mrs Fraser had found her voice again.

'I suppose we'd better be going,' she said weakly.

She went in to see Granny for a few minutes, then

they left, with Alexander. Mrs Fraser watched him put on his anorak and pick up the rucksack with a kind of stunned wonder. I did not doubt that she would recover strength later and let Catriona know what she thought of her little ploy.

'See you in the morning, Maggie,' said James.

'I thought we might have all gone up on the hills tomorrow,' said his mother. 'I'm sure Maggie could spare you for one day, couldn't you, dear?'

'You can all go,' said James, and added wickedly, 'Alexander can take my place.'

Alexander was picking up his skis. They looked brand new and must have cost a fortune.

'Have you done any skiing, Alexander?' asked Mr Fraser in a friendly voice.

'A bit.'

'You'll be lucky to get any just now, you know,' said Mrs Fraser tartly. 'It's too early.'

They seemed bound for a delightful evening, and although I was happy to be with my granny, I was sorry that I was going to miss it.

I went into Granny's room and sat beside the bed.

'They're away then, are they?' I nodded, and she said, 'Yon Jamie's an awful nice lad.'

CHAPTER TWELVE

JAMES WAS unable to spend every minute of every day with me, for obvious reasons, but even when he was not there I could think about him just by looking out towards the hills. The sight of them was a temptation: I wanted to get up and go there, to take the road to the glen winding between the forest and then along the lochside, and, gradually, as I would draw closer and closer the hills would be changing shape and getting bigger and higher. Snow had started to fall the day after we arrived and continued to drift down gently on to the stone cold ground where it lay, soft and clean, looking like cotton wool. The world was so bright that it startled me when I opened the curtains in the morning. It was the first time I had ever been so far north in winter.

My days were busy. I cooked and cleaned and tended Granny. My mother would have been astounded at this me, so domesticated, or at least able to be when I had to. And I had to: there was no choice. I cooked not only for Granny but usually for Mr Farquharson too, who normally fed poorly, sometimes also for Mrs Clark, who confessed that, living alone, she often did not bother to cook very much and lived off tea and buns. Then there was James.

'He has a big appetite, that laddie,' said Granny with approval. She hated poor eaters, thought a man who didn't eat well wasn't 'worth his salt'.

She made steady progress and was soon allowed up to sit by the fire for a little while every morning and afternoon. It was funny for me to see her sitting there in her nightie and dressing gown and a pair of brown carpet slippers. I always imagined her in overall and boots. The district nurse had brought her the slippers and dressing gown: she had never bothered about things like that before. They were unnecessary articles, by her way of thinking. When you got up in the morning you put your clothes on and no nonsense. My mother, who often had her dressing gown on till the middle of the morning, would have scandalised her. Shameless hussy! My mother and my granny have little in common, except my father.

'And what about your dad?' asked Granny. 'When is he coming to see his old mother?'

'He said he'd be up at Easter.'

She humphed. She'd believe it when she saw him. And when he did come he'd be away so quick afterwards you'd think someone was holding a match to his trousers.

'He doesn't like the glen now, Granny. He's got used to Glasgow.'

Och aye, she knew that all right! Anything to do with the town to her was bad, and it was useless to argue with her. The streets were running with wickedness. In her mind Glasgow was something like London in Dickens's time: men beating up their wives on street corners, mothers drinking gin, kids going barefoot and in tatters, thieving and begging from passers-by. She was not exactly *au fait* with the modern world.

'He's no the man his father was,' she said with a sigh.

She was probably right there but that did not mean that he was either better or worse than his father. He was just different. As I would be from my mother. I tried to make this point to Granny.

'I hope you'll be different from your mother, Maggie,' she said, and for a moment I was mad with her for I wasn't going to let anyone, even my granny, run my mother down. I might do it myself, but that's a different matter entirely. 'Keep your hair on, I'm no running her down. I ken she's probably all right in her own way.' But certainly not in Granny's way. 'She's a good enough woman and I'm sure she's made Andrew a good wife.'

'And you are a narrow-minded woman,' I snapped at Granny and flounced off into the kitchen where I began to bang pots around and talk to myself about the inadequacies of one's relations. Granny thought that anyone who didn't get up at six in the morning, cook her own porridge and broth and work twelve hours a day was soft.

The back door opened, in came James. I subsided.

I took Granny a cup of tea and a piece of her senna-coloured shortbread.

'Have you calmed off then? You've a fine temper on you, lass.' She chuckled. 'Just like I had when I was younger. I canne be bothered losing it now. It doesne seem worth it.'

'I'm glad,' I said, with sarcasm that was wasted. 'You're a real trial to me and I hope you know it, Granny McKinley!'

'I ken fine. You let me know it often enough.'

James had come in behind me. He said, 'Is she giving you a rough time, Mrs McKinley?'

'She is that. Come away and sit by the fire, Jamie, and get a wee warm to yourself.'

James sat down at the other side of the fire, I went to make broth in the kitchen. A woman's place! Well, I didn't mind being in the kitchen from time to time as long as I could do other things in life as well. I sang as I chopped onions and carrots.

The next day was Hogmanay. Granny gave me money from her purse in the sideboard – she'd been putting some by from her pension for the occasion – to go and get in a few necessities. Some food and drink. No good Scots housewife would be without plenty of both to offer visitors at New Year. The shops were busy with people who had come in from the whole area round about to load up with supplies for the next few days. Shops close for longer at New Year than Christmas in Scotland. There was a mood of excitement and gaiety about. My kind of mood. I don't go all that much for regular everyday routine. It is at times like these that I feel myself coming alive, my whole body seems to get an extra zing, and I could have danced up and down the street in spite of the slippy pavements and keen wind. The wind was powerfully cold coming straight off those white hills. When I came back to Granny's warm sitting room my nose was a delicate shade of cherry.

'Maggie the red-nosed reindeer,' I sang, as I unpacked the bag and set the bottles on the sideboard.

'You'll need to clean the house, mind,' Granny told me. 'I canne see the year in dirty.'

'I know, I know!' I was fully resigned to a full-scale house cleaning programme with her directing me, even though she herself had lived for the last ten years in her cottage in a state that was far from being described as clean. Her failing eyes might not be able to detect dirt but they could still ascertain whether I was washing the kitchen floor, vacuuming the sitting room carpet, polishing the furniture and cleaning the windows. I had never worked so hard in my life. By eight o'clock in the evening I was filthy and exhausted. I went to have a bath.

I lay and soaked for such a long time that in the end Granny came chapping at the bathroom door to see if I was all right. When I emerged, rosy-ish and my skin shrivelled from over-long submergence, she delivered me a lecture on the dangers of staying too long in hot water. It was a risk she couldn't have been said to run for she had never been all that partial to bodily submergence. For the most part of her life she had washed in an old zinc hip bath. Ghastly thing! Some aspects of modern life are for the better, I told her.

She looked at me wrapped as I was in a towel and nothing else.

'Gey few,' she answered. 'You'd better get yourself dressed, lass, before our visitors come.'

My green velvet dress was hanging in her bedroom. I had put it in my suitcase at the last moment and now I was glad for I decided that it was the ideal thing for me to wear to see the New Year in. It might mark the start of a new me, more sophisticated, more elegant, more mature. I took a while to dress, spraying on perfume, making up my eyes, brushing my hair which

140

usually takes one minute flat at the most to fix. Then I pinned on my Cairngorm brooch.

When I floated into the sitting room Granny sat back in surprise. 'Why, Maggie, you're looking fair bonny!' It sounded as if she had never considered it to be even a remote possibility before. 'Yon gown does things for you. And I see you're wearing the brooch.' She nodded with pleasure.

Mr Farquharson seemed equally surprised when he set eyes on me. He shifted about uncomfortably in his chair for the first five minutes eyeing me as if I were a stranger.

'It's all right, Mr Farquharson, I'm no imposter.' I gave him a glass of port and a piece of black bun which is a kind of heavy fruit cake wrapped in thick pastry.

'It's good bun, this,' he said chomping on it busily. He turned to Granny. 'Did you make it then, Mistress? My good wife made the finest black bun in the country when she was alive. God rest her soul!' He looked mournful for a moment, then resumed eating.

Mrs Clark arrived next, twittering and gleaming in sequined black. 'Just a little thing I bought when I was last in Edinburgh. Do you like it, Maggie?'

Lying in my teeth, I said that I did. How can you keep to the strict honesty bit in that kind of situation? She was dying to be admired and Mr Farquharson wasn't going to do it. Mrs Clark said she'd have a wee whisky, with no water, thank you. Granny had heard that she was not averse to a tipple from the bottle fairly regularly. Poor soul, she was probably lonely sitting up there in her tiny flat, with the only place to go being the grocer's or the chemist. Even the café closed in

141

winter time. The skiing business hadn't got here yet. A bit too far from the high hills.

Two other pensioners came in. They were not great talkers but they enjoyed sitting in the corner sipping their drinks and nibbling shortbread and listening to Mrs Clark and me talk about clothes. Mrs Clark adored clothes and wanted to know what was new in the shops in Glasgow. Anything I didn't know I invented to keep her happy since I was no expert on the subject and had had little time of late to case shop windows.

It was going on eleven by the time the Frasers arrived. With Alexander. So he was still surviving!

'Hope we're not too late,' cried Mrs Fraser, bustling in laden with stuff. Bottles and bags, and a big box of chocolates. 'But we had an enormous meal rather late and by the time we sat over it – Well, you know how time flies!'

The pensioners stared at her. Her breeziness was quite alien to them, apart from Mrs Clark, who liked a bit of hubbub. She blossomed and twittered anew, and her fingers fluttered happily over the chocolate box when it was offered to her. Ah, violet creams! How delicious!

The small room was crowded now. We young ones sat on the floor, the rest managed somehow. Granny sat by the fire in her own chair smiling, her hands clasped on her lap. It was just like the old times in the glen, she told me later, before everybody moved out; they had always gathered in her cottage on Hogmanay and many's the wild night they'd had, singing and dancing till dawn. There'd be no singing and dancing here tonight but we did plenty of eating, drinking and talking.

At midnight we paused and Mr Fraser proposed the toast. We raised our glasses, cried 'Happy New Year!' and drank, then we all kissed one another, even the old folk. It was exciting to think that there was a new year born. A new chance to do things better. I was going to try to cultivate patience: that was my main resolution.

Alexander was our First Foot since he had black hair. Granny made him go outside and come back in with a lump of coal in his hand, then she was happy. No chance of bad luck now! Shortly afterwards the grocer from the village and his wife called, then the chemist looked in, and the baker, and the district nurse. We spilled over into the kitchen and the hallway.

At one o'clock Mrs Fraser said that Granny looked very tired and it was time they were going. I could not argue against that for Granny did seem done in, but the thought of all that gaiety and fun disappearing just when I was getting going sobered me.

The pensioners, other than Mrs Clark, were ready for their beds too. But she said, 'It's been a lovely, lovely evening and I have enjoyed myself,' and off she tripped after the others.

The Frasers were putting on their coats, all but James who was holding my hand.

'Come on now, James,' said his mother. 'Maggie wants to get her granny into bed.'

'It's too bad for the lassie to have to go to her bed at this hour on a New Year's morn,' said Granny. 'Could she no go back to the glen with you, Mrs Fraser? I'd be fine on my own now.'

'Well, I don't know if you should be left alone,' said Mrs Fraser.

'I'm usually on my ain and I manage fine, you ken

that. And I'm ill no longer, just a wee bitty tired. I have a bell by my bed to ring if I'm needing help, and Mrs Clark's only up the stairs.'

'That's a great idea!' said James. 'Maggie coming, I mean. If you're sure you'll be all right, Mrs McKinley?'

Granny was very sure; in fact, she said she would as soon I went and stayed away a day or so, for she could be doing with her house to herself for a while.

'You ken when Maggie's here the house is aye full of folk. She's like a magnet.'

Before we went I helped Granny into bed.

'Thanks, Gran.'

She winked at me. 'I kent fine you were pining to see a bit more of your laddie.'

I was not only pining for that, but for a look at my glen. Yes, *my* glen. That was how it was now. As we drove out there, under the clear, starry sky, I felt so excited that I thought I might go through the roof of the car. There was some literal danger of that too, for to get us all squashed into the Frasers' small car I had to sit on James's knee. Not that he nor I minded. Only one person did. But since there was no other alternative, apart from me riding in the boot or on the roof, she couldn't say anything. Mr Fraser said that, now that the children were fully grown and their family seemed to be expanding, it might be a good idea to buy a station wagon or a caravanette? Mrs received his idea in silence.

Even though it was dark I knew and recognised each corner, every twist in the road, and when we came round the last bend into the glen and saw the white mountains rising out of the darkness on either side I whooped with joy. I couldn't help it!

We stepped out. The road glittered with cold, our breath froze in front of us. The air was as pure as a big drink of ice-cold water. I looked across the road and saw that the gutted remains of my granny's cottage still stood though Mr Fraser had heard that someone had bought the land from the Forestry Commission and was planning to build a holiday cottage on it.

It was warm in the Frasers' sitting room for they had a big closed stove that they kept on night and day during their winter visits. Mrs Fraser opened the door and we sat in front of it to warm up and drink hot chocolate. Catriona put some music on; she and Alexander got up to dance. I eyed James but he was not keen on dancing, especially under his mother's eye. Alexander and Catriona danced in and out of the shadows, staying well away from the lighted part of the room. Mrs Fraser kept glancing with troubled eyes at Alexander. I daresay last New Year had been better, from her point of view; there would just have been the four of them and no nasty outsiders to upset the family peace and quiet.

Between three and four a.m. Mrs Fraser began to flag. Mr had gone to sleep and was snoring gently in his chair smiling every now and then as if he was having a good dream. I hoped he was. Once or twice her head drooped, then jerked up again. At last she woke her husband and said it was time for them to turn in.

'What about you young ones? Don't you think you should come too? Tomorrow's another day.'

'It's New Year, mother,' protested Catriona.

'She's right, Elizabeth,' said Mr Fraser, yawning.

'Let them stay up. They're young, they're not tired. We didn't used to be either, when we were their age.'

When they had gone James danced with me too. He was not smooth on his feet, as Alexander was, but once I got him going he managed not to kick me too often. Alexander relaxed with the removal of Catriona's parents; he allowed his hair to get ruffled, forgot to speak in a silly manner and became almost human. No doubt he was having a tough time. The atmosphere had apparently been strained, to say the least! He still smiled too much for my liking but I had decided it could be due to 'nerves'. But perhaps after my recent experience with my mother, I was too inclined to put things down to that. He might just have liked smiling.

We drew the curtains back from the big window before dawn and watched the light start to come into the sky. I wanted to see the very first touch of colour and I did, a suggestion, no more, of pink; then gradually it grew, rising higher and higher, becoming flame-red, and the other colours followed: turquoise, yellow, and blues of every shade. Watching the sky from this window with James had been one of my favourite pastimes at the glen. But the colours, with snow on the ground, were even brighter and more breathtaking.

'Let's go out!' said James.

I changed into jeans, sweater, anorak and boots. We charged out into the white morning, churning up snow like fluffy clouds under our feet. We ran when we did not slip and when we slipped we laughed and caught one another. Catriona and Alexander had decided to go out too but we lost track of them and went our own way. We went up to the head of the glen, all the way, and it did not seem so very long, even to me. Not a car passed us on the road, there was not a sign of a beast on the moors. Smoke had been puffing from the farm chimney as we passed but apart from that we might have been the only beings alive on the face of the earth. An exhilarating feeling!

At the head of the glen we climbed up a little way and rested on the side of the hill to look down and back. Almost everything was covered with white: the moors, the ruins of the old abandoned cottages with my great-great-granny's amongst them, the dry stane dykes, the few stunted trees that thrived here. Only the odd stone and branch had escaped the snow. But the sun had emerged and spread a golden light over the land.

We might have stayed out all day, except that we were starving. The trek back down the glen seemed longer but I did not complain, not too much, that is, knowing that I wouldn't get much sympathy. You mustn't grumble when you're out trekking with the Frasers; they're of the 'grin-and-bear-it' school. Even if they were hanging on to the north face of the Eiger by their toe-nails it would all be jolly good fun. And character building, needless to say.

'We've been wondering where you two were,' said Mrs Fraser, when we opened the kitchen door and staggered inside. Fatigue was catching up with us now. After all, we had not been to bed, and it was mid-morning. Alexander and Catriona had come back ages before and were sound asleep.

James and I peeled off our steaming top clothes and sat down to an enormous breakfast. By the time I was stuffed full I was just able to totter into my bunk below

Catriona, and within seconds must have slept, because the next thing I knew it was late afternoon. I got up in time to watch the sun set.

Mrs Fraser had cooked a fat goose for New Year's dinner, which she served with all the trimmings. If I didn't get beef on my bones this festive season then I never would! I could not remember ever having eaten so much. After dinner James, Catriona, Alexander and I went out and had a snowball fight in the dark to help shake the food down and make room for the nuts and sweetmeats on the fireside table. Alexander sulked a bit when he got a fat snowball – thrown by me – right inside his collar. He had to be coaxed round by Catriona. 'But I'm soaking,' he moaned. I had made a resolution to try to like him but was finding it hard going. I didn't *dislike* him: he just didn't turn me on. Not that I let it bother me.

It was a gorgeous New Year, except for one thing.

'I'll run you down to the phone box in the car,' said James.

He stayed in the car whilst I went into the box. There was no light in it but James had given me a torch so I managed to dial the operator. She connected me up quite quickly which was just as well for I'd have been stuck to the floor with cold if I'd had to wait any longer. Half the glass was missing, not because of vandals here, but old age.

My mother answered the phone. 'Is that you, Maggie? How are you, then? A Happy New Year to you!' She sounded a little tipsy, as well she might on New Year's night.

I wished her a Happy New Year and sent greetings

from my granny and the Frasers, then she called the rest of the family to the phone in turns. My father came first, sounding skittish, for him: and when I talked to him about Granny he got quite sentimental, telling me what a good mother she had been to them, how hard she had worked and sacrificed herself.

'You're lucky you have such a fine granny, Maggie.'

'She was wondering when you were coming to see her?'

'Aye well . . . you've told her how busy I am with the business and all that?'

I had promised him for Easter, I informed him. Okay, he'd be there! Then he passed the phone to Jean, who was in a giggly mood. A glass of sherry and she'll giggle all night. Her friend Lorraine was there too. Sandy shouted something from the background; he wasn't going to take the receiver into his hand and speak to his sister. There was a terrible racket going on, as if half the street was gathered in the flat, which it probably was. Aunt Jessie and Uncle Tam also came on the line to wish me a Happy New Year, and Aunt Jessie asked fondly after James.

'No news for us, dear?'

'What do you mean *news*?'

'Well, I mean to say, you and James – '

'James and I are only good friends.' It was difficult to sound haughty in an ice-cold box with my teeth chattering and the wind whistling round my feet. 'And I am only sixteen, Aunt Jessie!'

'What's that?'

'Sixteen,' I yelled down the phone. 'And not very sweet.'

'You'll be seventeen in March. I married your Uncle Tam when I was seventeen.'

'Good for you.' This was a ridiculous conversation to be having, given the circumstances. I put in my third lot of money. This was costing me a fortune.

I said goodbye to Aunt Jessie, had another quick word with my mother and then everyone at the other end gathered to shriek 'Happy New Year' at me. The noise was deafening and I had to remove the receiver well away from my head to preserve my ear-drum.

The door needed a good shove to get it opened. The cold was making everything stick, and James himself, usually so hardy, was blowing on his hands when I got back into the car. He started up the engine at once.

'They all send love and best wishes and all that.'

'Good. How are they?'

'Steaming.'

He laughed. For a few minutes I had felt so homesick that I could have turned and run for Glasgow but by the time we arrived back at the cottage I was over it. You usually can't have everything you want, not all at once. I thought I was pretty lucky as it was.

CHAPTER THIRTEEN

WE STAYED ten days in Inverness-shire altogether. The rest of the holiday just seemed to slip by. I went back to Granny on the second of January. James came to see me every day and twice he fetched me to spend a few hours in the glen. The snow was unusually good for skiing that year, and the Frasers, mostly without James, headed for the ski slopes as often as they could. Catriona and Alexander had arranged to take their winter week's holiday from work, which put Mrs Fraser back further, for she had expected that Alexander would only have the statutory holiday of three days and then return to Edinburgh.

The morning after their first ski outing, James arrived grinning. 'You should have seen Mother's face yesterday! Alexander is a fantastic skier. She had been telling him all the way there how and how not to ski – you know what she's like, she had to give advice – and then when we got there he went sailing off as if he'd been born with skis on his feet.' He became a different person. He had been sure of himself, I suppose, and that had made the difference. He had learned to ski at school, an Edinburgh state school, for Edinburgh schoolchildren get a chance to learn on the artificial ski slope on the Pentland Hills. So Mrs Fraser was revising her opinion of Alexander and the next time I saw them together she was trying to be nice to him. She so much approves of people who are good at sports and keen on the wide open spaces that she seems to think they have a kind of purity which the rest of us poor unenlightened mortals lack. I said so to James.

'But *you* like wide open spaces.'

Yes, that was true, though it had not come to me all that naturally, and I felt my approach was somewhat different from Mrs Fraser's.

'You'll have to learn to ski, Maggie,' said Mr Fraser.

'Not me. I'd break a leg, or my neck. Both would be inconvenient.'

'Nonsense, you'd love it,' said James. 'It's exhilarating. You can start at Easter. The snow's usually still good then.'

Easter? Mrs Fraser's ears pricked. She did not like the sound of that. Was she never going to have another holiday without me?

The idea of going skiing with the Frasers was unnerving. There they would be skiing effortlessly and gracefully, making beautiful patterns on the snow and all that jazz, and there would I be floundering about the wrong way up half the time, breaking ski poles and legs and generally disturbing the peace. No, no, I knew my limitations.

'At Easter you shall learn how to ski,' said James with determination.

'It won't be long till Easter,' I said to Granny as I packed my bag. The term would pass quickly, I had plenty to do. At the end of last term Mr Scott had said he hoped I would do a lot of work during the holidays, and he had meant studying, not doing Granny and Mr Farquharson's laundry, cooking and shopping for half the residents in the flats. I had read a couple of books, one on the Albiri Aborigines of Central Australia, the other on the Sea Dayaks of Borneo, neither of which was much help with my immediate schoolwork. And once I managed to open a biology textbook before I fell asleep in front of the fire. That is one of the complications about spending hours in the great outdoors: you come indoors and can hardly keep your eyes open.

Alexander went home on the train, the Frasers collected me.

'Take care of yourself, Gran now. And I'll be back at Easter, remember!'

'Bring that father of yours with you.'

I nodded. Quickly I said goodbye, then left. She watched us go from the window, as did Mrs Clark and Mr Farquharson and a few others, from their windows. 'It'll be gey quiet when you're gone, Maggie,' Granny had said the night before.

'She's looking fine now, Maggie,' said Mrs Fraser. 'You've done her a lot of good.'

That was what she told my mother and father too when we arrived in Glasgow. 'I don't know what old Mrs McKinley would do without Maggie,' she said. She was always a bit disapproving of my father for not going more often to see his mother. She didn't seem to realise that he had short holidays compared with her and Mr Fraser so he didn't have much time to himself.

James and I agreed that we could not expect to see much of one another between now and Easter. His eighteenth birthday fell at the end of the month and I was to go to Edinburgh then, and he would come to Glasgow at the beginning of March for my seventeenth birthday. We had agreed too that we would not gripe about it, that we must make the best of it. Agreeing is the easy bit; it's what comes after that's difficult.

We stood in the back shop saying goodbye, delaying the moment of parting, and outside in the car sat the other three Frasers trying not to look round, no doubt, or be impatient.

'You must go,' I said.

We kissed again, and then I walked with him to the car.

'Thanks for everything,' I said to the Frasers.

I watched them drive off. James waved until I could no longer see him. It was raining of course, I might have known that it would be, and doubtless, up there, in the frozen north, snow would be falling, softly, soundlessly. The silence was another thing that had startled me, along with the brilliance. Here the roar of the traffic was tearing at my ears.

'Come in at once, Maggie,' shouted my mother from the upstairs window. 'You'll get soaked if you stand there gawping any longer.'

So it was back to work, both at school and home. Unknown to me, until afterwards, Mr Scott came round and had a talk with my mother and father and told them that they must not impose on me and expect me to do so much in the business.

'I told him I want you to get your Highers too,' said my father, who was a bit pipped by it.

'He was awful nice about it, mind,' said my mother. 'And it is true, you know, Andrew, the lassie doesne get all that much time to herself.'

My father sighed. 'Aye, well you're to get on with your school work now. I'm no wanting to waste all this money keeping you for nothing.'

'Now, Andrew!' said my mother. 'She's always been a credit to us, you ken that.'

He was not going to make a speech of appreciation on my behalf, and I did not expect it. The moon would turn blue before that happened, but I knew he was proud of me in his own way.

January and February were difficult months for the business. Money is always tight at the start of the year, said Aunt Jessie, for folk have broken the bank to pay for Christmas and the New Year. People don't think of replumbing or putting in new bathrooms at this time of year. They don't want to buy cloth animals either. About the only work going was repairing burst pipes. My father and uncle sat in the back shop playing cards again; we ate sausages and beans on toast and my mother and father ate tripe which Sandy, Jean and I absolutely refuse to touch. We don't know what's good for us, my mother says every time she serves up the revolting greyish-white mess. I'd rather eat grass than the lining of a sheep's stomach.

'Aye, well you might end up eating grass,' said my father. 'If things don't pick up come the spring, your Uncle Tam and I'll be bankrupt.'

At the end of January I duly went to Edinburgh. James was having a party for his birthday, a large one with about forty people. His mother had been busy for days, as had his father who had been redecorating the drawing room for the occasion. It was a fair task for the room was like a ballroom, with three long windows, and a ceiling about fifteen feet high.

Mrs Fraser had fussed, and Catriona and I dashed up and down the kitchen being scullions without a murmur of protest. We laid out a fantastic cold buffet of meats, fowls, salads, trifles, fruits and cakes in the dining room.

'So James is coming of age,' said Grandfather Fraser, who sat back with a serene smile and watched everyone scurrying like mad ants.

'I still think of twenty-one as the real coming of age,' said James's mother.

'But he does get the vote,' said Grandfather. 'If a man can vote then he must be considered full grown.'

'Hear, hear!' said James. 'So be warned, Mother, no more bullying me!'

'A mother is entitled to bully her children all her life,' said Grandfather, 'so you can't expect to escape that, James. Anyway, your mother doesn't bully. She merely shows concern for you.'

He was a silver-tongued lawyer right enough, but I enjoyed his talk and whenever I could I slipped away from the kitchen and joined him by the fire in his small sitting room.

The party was a great success, and Mrs Fraser was happy. So was Mr Fraser who was in charge of the punch bowl. I had met a number of the guests at the Frasers' Boxing Day party so did not feel the odd one out. Alexander was invited, too, so Catriona was all right. Her mother might have admired him as a skier but she was obviously still not sure about any other aspect of him. From time to time I caught her giving her daughter and Alexander an uneasy glance, and no doubt there were times when she cast uneasy glances in James's and my direction also.

My birthday would not be nearly such a grand affair; in fact, I did not intend to have a party at all. We have never gone in much for birthday parties in our family, usually just having a rather special tea with maybe one or two friends as well. I had always had Isobel in; this year I did not. We had seen so little of one another that it would have been odd to suddenly invite her, and the only friend I really wanted to have was James. I told my mother that I would make the meal, she need not bother herself. After poring through recipe books in the library I decided on Chicken Morocco. My father wouldn't like it, he'd make a face and push his plate away for he couldn't stand spicy things, but I decided he would have to lump it. He was not the one I was making it for.

My mother said that James could sleep on the settee in the sitting room if he wanted to. There was no need for him to go round to the Scotts.

'Could he?' I was pleased, for this was the first time she had ever suggested it.

'I'm not wanting the Scotts to think we won't put up your friend ourselves. Tell him he's welcome.' She paused for a moment, then said, 'Maggie, how serious are you with this laddie?' I shrugged, and she added, 'You haven't looked at another boy since last summer.'

'I haven't had time.'

'That's no the only reason I'm thinking.'

Why did adults always try to push your life on too fast? I asked her, and she said she wasn't pushing, she was only thinking of my welfare. That's always the story, with parents!

'You see, Maggie, if you're just going to end up getting married I think you'd be as well leaving school at the end of this year.'

Suffering doughnuts, how many times did I have to have this conversation! At the end of it my mother never did seem to get the whole message: that an education and a career were not a waste for a woman even if she got married and had twenty children. I shuddered at the very idea of that. Whenever I saw children *en masse* I had doubts about my maternal instincts. Janet Scott laughed when I told her.

'You don't feel maternal except for your own.'

'I don't want to think about my own.' I had come round to the Scotts to get away from that. They were always my refuge when my family got too much for me.

'How's the work going?' asked Mr Scott.

'All right.' I was working every night until midnight, going to bed stiff-shouldered, hot-eyed, and my head so full of stuff that at times I found it difficult to shut off.

'You're young,' said Mrs Scott. 'You'll survive.'

'Huh!'

James was studying hard too. We exchanged moans on the telephone. Mrs Fraser had had a bill in that had made her explode so now we limited ourselves to ten minutes at a time.

The week-end of my birthday came, bringing James into Queen Street Station. He was laden with gifts from his family for me.

'Isn't that real nice of them?' said Aunt Jessie, who came to the shop that day, not so much because it was my birthday but because James would be there. I was glad she was as old as she was, otherwise she might have been competition for me. She exclaimed over every gift as if it was part of the Crown Jewels, particularly a ceramic pendant sent by James's mother. 'They must think an awful lot of Maggie to send all this to her?'

'Oh, they do,' said James. 'An awful lot.'

We spent a lovely day together, all on our own. We went into town, had lunch and then drifted about the streets, a thing I had not done for a long time but used to do for hours in my ill-spent youth, usually arriving home late to a tirade from my mother who had been nearly up the wall wondering which horrible fate I had succumbed to out of the long list of possibilities she kept in her mind. I showed James various nooks and crannies, old haunts of Isobel's and mine, and we went to the Botanic Gardens – Glaswegian version.

'We have good things in Glasgow too, you know.'

'I do know. Very good things.'

We were so idiotic that everywhere we went we usually ended up like a couple of statues staring at one another with silly grins. We frequently got in other people's ways.

When we returned home I put the finishing touches to my cuisine and got James to open the wine.

'Doing things in style, aren't you?' said my father, eyeing the two bottles on the draining board. He was still worried about money matters.

'Present from James's grandfather.'

That silenced my father and when his North African chicken was set before him he passed no remarks but began to eat and did not cease until his plate was cleared, kept at it perhaps by the thought that the chicken might have been a present from James's mother.

'You're no a bad wee cook when you try,' said my mother.

'She's just about burnt the mouth off me,' said Sandy getting up for a glass of water.

'Don't be so provincial,' I told him.

'Listen to her!' said Sandy.

I feared that Sandy and Jean were getting disrespectful towards me in James's company now that they were getting used to him. Until recently they had been unnaturally polite in his presence, but it would have been too much to hope that it would continue.

Sunday was one of those crisp sunny days when you felt that spring was hovering only a little way off. We went walking in the park and found some snowdrops with the same excitement that we might have discovered gold. We crouched in front of them. They looked so fragile it was difficult to believe they had pushed up through the cold hard ground.

'It won't be long till Easter, Maggie,' said James.

'No, not long.'

And when it did come then James and I would be together for two whole weeks.

CHAPTER FOURTEEN

I HAD a letter from Mrs Clark saying that Granny was doing fine and counting the days to my visit. I read it aloud to my parents at breakfast time.

'You're no thinking of going up there for your whole two weeks off are you?' asked my father.

'Yes, I was.' He looked glum, so I added, 'Why not?'

'I was hoping you might give me a hand with the business. I've been counting on it.'

'But Mum and Aunt Jessie manage fine between them. And Jean could help out too during the holidays.'

'It's not just a matter of minding the shop. You see, Maggie – I haven't said anything before because I haven't wanted to worry you while you were so busy with your studying – but we're not doing all that well at the moment. We're needing a bit of a boost. Quite a bit! And it's you we're needing to give us one.'

'Me?'

'Well, you know what you're like, you can aye think of something.' He leant his head on his hand, and his elbow on the table. 'You'll need to.' His arm sagged as if his head was a ball of lead.

'But you've had quite a lot of enquiries recently. I've taken a number myself.'

'Oh aye, we've done quite a few estimates. But we haven't been getting the jobs.'

'Then we have to find out why not.'

'That's right.'

'Can't you and Uncle Tam do that?'

'You know we haven't a great head for figures. Look, Maggie, you and I'll go up and see your granny for a week-end and then we'll come back down and get things sorted out here. I'll take the van up.'

I stormed and raged and said I would not do it. He could not make me. No, he agreed, he could not, but if the business flopped then we wouldn't have enough to eat, or money to pay the rent, electricity, telephone etc., and I would have to leave school and get a job. It was as bad as that, he said, and I should make no mistake about it.

'That's blackmail,' I cried. 'You're holding a gun to my head.'

'Do you think I want to? Do you think I want to go bankrupt?'

No, of course I did not, but what I did think was that he and Uncle Tam should be able to manage their affairs a bit better. On the other hand, I knew, and had known when I first suggested the idea, that, whereas they were good plumbers, neither of them were business men. They could go out on the job and do a good job but they needed someone to direct them, and neither my mother nor Aunt Jessie was capable of doing that either. It was a wild thing to consider that my father needed *me* to tell him what to do. For a moment I was intoxicated by the idea of my power and indispensability but that quickly subsided for I didn't want power of that kind and anyone knows that to be indispensable is a real drag. It cuts your freedom. And I wanted mine. I wanted it very much.

I raged again, against families, life in general, and the need for money. My mother said I always wanted everything, she didn't see why a week-end wouldn't do me. After all, I'd had the whole of the New Year holiday in Inverness-shire. She would not understand, I informed her, and went out to pound the pavements of Glasgow, returning only when I was exhausted.

When James phoned I said nothing about this new development because a part of me still refused to accept that I must spend my Easter vacation in Glasgow. I usually did manage to get what I wanted one way or another in the end, and I thought there must be a way round this problem. I started to study the books in the evenings but I had so much school work to do and there was so much to examine that I made little progress. Since Christmas I had not paid much attention to the shop books and saw that they were now in a muddle.

I would not be travelling north with the Frasers this time; they were going a day ahead of us and I told James that I would see him at my granny's. His mother said that I could sleep at the cottage whilst my father was at Granny's since she had so little space in her flat.

The night before we were due to leave I went round to see the Scotts. I told them my troubles.

'What would you do?' I asked.

'Just what you're going to do,' said Mrs Scott.

I sighed.

'I think Maggie's family asks too much of her,' said Janet.

'That's the way of families,' said Mr Scott. 'And what else can Maggie do? They've laid off during term time, I must admit that, and Maggie hasn't had a day off school. Yes, I know, your mother's kept Jean off instead when she needed someone!'

'Oh, well, you're young, Maggie,' said Janet. 'You'll have plenty of chances to spend holidays in Inverness-shire.'

'That's what my mother said.'

Janet looked taken aback for a moment, then laughed. 'I suppose it did sound a bit elderly.'

'I am young,' I said, feeling at that moment at least ninety-five. 'But my granny is not.'

But it was not only my granny I was thinking of.

My father and I left in the van at first light on the Friday morning. He fussed as if we were driving to the North Pole. My mother, in dressing-gown and rollers, waved us off from the shop doorway, calling out last minute instructions and warnings. Watch out for ice, fog and flying saucers! I was sure she'd think of a few more hazards as soon as we'd turned the corner.

We didn't talk much on the journey. My father never talks much at the best of times and when he's driving he likes to concentrate on the road. I watched the scenery unfold, still mostly bare as at New Year, but sprouting a little here and there, a few budding trees showing promise of spring; and I thought of my granny and of James.

We arrived at Granny's in the early afternoon, about two hours earlier than my father had forecast. He believes in allowing himself a good leeway.

'Well, Andrew,' said Granny, 'so you made it after all.'

As usual he became all meek and mild in her presence and allowed her to scold him and take him to task for not writing, not coming and so forth. At the end of it she said she was glad enough to see him and he should sit down and stop dithering about. When he came north he was always restless, not knowing where to put himself. He had the look on his face of a guilty schoolboy.

Shortly after we arrived the district nurse came to give Granny her bath. 'I tell you what,' said Granny, 'you take Maggie to the glen, Andrew, whilst I'm having my bath. I ken by the look in her eye she's halfway there already.'

My father agreed reluctantly. I was torn between Granny and James, and she did not know yet that I would not be staying for the two weeks I had planned.

'Okay,' I said. 'I'll be back tomorrow morning, Gran.'

'That'll be grand. I'll have your father to myself for a wee while.'

My father drove the road to the glen slowly. He must have known it well, had walked it so many times as a child and a youth. They used to go to *ceilidhes* in the town, walking there and back without thinking anything of it. He had told me so often when I had griped about walking the odd mile.

When we came to the churchyard by the loch where his father and ancestors are buried, he stopped. He got out of the car without a word. I followed. We walked into the cemetery and made for the family grave. We stood in front of it looking at the names. His father Andrew, the forester. His granny. And my granny's granny, Margaret Ross: she who had come from Greenyards, in Easter Ross.

'We should have brought some flowers,' he said.

'Difficult to get up here at this time of year.'

'Aye.'

It was peaceful and very quiet. He did not tell me what he was thinking. He never would. We left the cemetery and continued to the glen. As we rounded the corner and the black remains of Granny's cottage came into view he drew in his breath sharply. It had been there that he had been born and grew up, had lived until he was ready to go off and seek his fortune in the big city. Some fortune! I could hear my mother's voice in the background.

'I think we'll just take a wee run up to the head of the glen,' he said.

We drove to the end, he switched off the engine and sat looking at the bare hills.

'Are you coming out?' I said.

'It looks gey chilly out there.'

'Come on, just for a minute.'

We climbed a little way up the brown heather, my father puffing and panting with the exertion.

'I'm fair out of shape,' he said, as he rested with his foot against a rock. 'I used to be able to run up there and along the ridge, no bother.' He looked down the glen. 'It's a dreich place.' He shook his head.

I protested. 'It's beautiful!'

'But empty. What can a man do here?'

'Didn't you like it when you were a boy?'

'I never thought about it. I didn't know anything else.'

We went back to the car, drove back along to the Frasers' cottage. I was pleased I had come with my father to the glen for although he had not said much I had felt closer to him than I had ever done. I felt, too, that the visit had been important to him, even though he had not wanted to come in the first place.

The Frasers were at home.

'Are you coming in, Mr McKinley?' asked Mrs.

'No, no thanks, I'll be getting back to my mother.' He backed away. 'See you in the morn, Maggie.'

James was so pleased to see me that I could not tell him my stay was to be so short. We might as well have one clear day, or part day, for that was all that was left, before I broke the news. Catriona was not with them for she did not get an Easter holiday from work. She would get one day off for the Edinburgh spring holiday. We pagan Scots do not keep religious holidays, not publicly at any rate.

'We've left Catriona and Father to look after one another,' said Mr Fraser.

'She could be swinging from the chandeliers and he wouldn't notice,' said Mrs.

Mr smiled. 'True. He tends to see only what he can be bothered to see.'

'Just like my granny,' I said. 'She's as deaf as a post when it suits her, and when it doesn't her ears sharpen up remarkably.' Added to that, she had some kind of sixth sense which made up for any lack of sight or hearing so that nothing really important passed her by.

James and I spent the rest of the afternoon in the woods and along the burn-side. We found some snow-drops and one or two early crocuses. Things were later

167

here than in Glasgow but we saw spikes of green pushing upward and even one or two birds that had returned
to build their nests.

'I thought the last three months would never end,'
said James. 'I only got through them by thinking that
we would have this holiday together. What's the matter,
Maggie? Aren't you pleased to be here?'

'Of course. You know I love the glen.'

'And me? What about me?' His tone was jocular,
but serious underneath.

'You're not so bad,' I said, and then cried, 'Look,
there goes a hare! A mad March hare.'

We saw it scamper through the half-light. The sky
was darkening, the hills changing with it, and the air
cooling. We clung together, turned for the road and
headed back for the lighted cottage.

We played Scrabble in the evening after supper, and
when Mr and Mrs Fraser went off to bed she let us
stay to watch the fire die down. We promised that we
would not stay longer.

'The day after tomorrow I am going to take you
to the ski run,' said James.

I looked at his face in the flickering firelight. He
looked so happy and contented that my heart contrac-
ted. I felt it in a physical way. I could no longer stall,
keep back my news. I had to tell him.

'You're going home the day after tomorrow?' he
said slowly.

I nodded. 'I don't want to but I've got to.'

'You haven't got to! You can refuse.'

'My father needs me, James.'

'I need you.'

'It's not the same thing.'

'No, it's not. My need is more important.' He sounded pompous.

'You can't say that. Don't be silly, don't be angry.'

But he was angry, very angry, and I had never seen him so before, not in that cold, hard way. He said that I had promised these two weeks to him and I must tell my family so. I was too much at their beck and call and I must stand up to them for his sake. He had had to stand up to his mother for my sake. Did I not know that? Did I not know that he and his mother had had rows over me, but he had never wavered, he had always said I was important to him and he would not let her get between us. But what about me? Here was I letting my family get between us and spoil our holiday together! Was I just a weakling who would let herself be pushed around? He didn't believe it; he believed I could do anything I wanted. So maybe I didn't want to spend the two weeks with him? Maybe this was just an excuse, this story of having to save the business from bankruptcy.

It was no story, I cried, it was only too real, and I wished it were not. Now I was furious, at his lack of sympathy and his selfishness. I told him so, in no uncertain terms. The row built and built until it got out of all proportion. And when it comes to getting out of proportion no one can hold a candle to me. I know that afterwards, that's the funny thing, but at the time I feel fully justified in saying the most outrageous things. Something inside me says, 'Careful', but whatever it is I find it dead easy to ignore.

James Fraser, you are selfish, self-centred and self-opinionated, and I hate you.

James Fraser, you are so possessive, you think you have

some right of ownership over me, but you have nothing, and you never will!

James Fraser, you are so arrogant.

You are so stupid.

You are so ignorant. You do not know how the other half of the world lives. You with your fee-paying school and your Georgian house and your rich grandfather!

You are a snob. You think my family is beneath you. In my eyes you are beneath them.

James Fraser, you are so nice, so polite. And always smiling! What a nice lad says my granny, says my Aunt Jessie, says my mother even and there are usually no fleas on her. They don't know you! Oh no they don't, not one bit.

He said a few things to me too, when he could get a word in edgeways, which I did my best to prevent: about me being stubborn, wild-tempered, thrawn (he'd got that from my granny), infuriating, wayward, and one or two other charges which no one could take seriously. Certainly not me.

That was it then! We were finished! He nodded: he agreed. I turned my back to him. I was trembling.

I got up and went to bed; he did not come. And I did not go. I had my pride.

In the morning we were stone-faced to one another. His mother was astounded, opened her mouth and quickly closed it, obviously getting the message. I glanced at James across the breakfast table and hated him. His face looked as if it had been chipped out of granite. I drank only a cup of tea, ate nothing.

'I have to get back to my granny's,' I said. I looked at Mr Fraser. 'I wonder – '

'Would you like a lift?' He tried to sound normal,

but failed. In the car, he said, 'It's no business of mine, but I suppose you've had a tiff?' I nodded. 'It happens to everyone, you know, Maggie. I'm sure – '

'James and I are finished!'

I explained to his father why I had to go back to Glasgow. He understood straight away, said *he* was sorry. *He* was more understanding than James.

'I hope you'll get your business affairs sorted out, Maggie. Listen, if you need any advice, go and see my father. He'd be only too delighted to help you. He's very fond of you.' Then he added, kind of gruffly, 'We all are.' He dropped me in front of my granny's house. 'See you soon, I expect. I hope.'

There was a big lump lodged somewhere at the back of my throat as I watched his car drive away.

I could feel myself quivering as I walked into the living room where Granny and my father were having a late breakfast in front of the fire.

'What's up with you, lass?' asked Granny. 'You've a face on you like a dreich day at the back end of November.'

I burst into tears, astonishing them. Jean is the one in my family who gives way to tears, they spill out of her like a fountain being switched on. But I, Maggie McKinley, am seldom known to cry, and when I do, I try not to do it in front of an audience.

My father got up in alarm. 'What's happened?' He was thinking in terms of accidents, sudden deaths, things like that.

I shook my head but could not bring out a word. I fled into Granny's room and flung myself face downwards on the bed. She hobbled in after me, closing the door behind her. Her sixth sense told her this was woman's concern and we did not need my father.

'Now then, lass, you can tell me.' I felt her rough hand stroke my hair.

I sat up, blew my nose hard and was then able to tell her, though not the full details. I could not let either her or my father know why James and I had quarrelled.

'Ah well, you ken what they say about true love?'

'But I don't even know if this is true love.'

'Why else would you be in such a state?'

I did not think she was necessarily right there but I did not argue. She said that James would come, I'd see, and before the night'd fall we'd have made it up.

'I have to go in the morning, Gran.'

'I know. Your father told me,' she said calmly. She was better at accepting things than me. She had more experience. 'You'll come in the summer?'

'For the whole summer!'

If that was possible. I *must* make it possible.

I did not move far from Granny's house that day and when I did go to the shops I hurried back, but as I came through the door each time Granny shook her head.

'Now, dinne fret, lass, he'll come. There's time yet. And he's a proud lad too, he'll no come running easily.'

I worked all day, unable to sit. Mr Farquharson had been saving his washing for me, a great mountain of dirty clothes which he had pushed under the bed, perhaps in the hope it would disappear. Or maybe he thought the fairies would come in the night and do it for him?

172

'Oh I wouldne laugh at the wee folk, Maggie. Many's the dealings I've had with them in my life.' He nodded his head wisely. And who was I to say whether he had ever seen fairies or not? I toiled over the washing that they had neglected to do and strung it out in the crisp breeze. When I had pegged out the last nightshirt (they looked as if they had survived from the Boer War) I turned and looked at the hills. There was snow on them. Had James gone skiing? Was he missing me? Was he sad? Or was he relieved to be shot of me? I still hated him with a fury that burned brightly inside me but at the same time I wanted more than anything else to see him come up the path with his long smooth stride, watch the smile break on his face and hear his voice say my name. Idiot McKinley! Forget him! He isn't worth it.

We switched on the light but I wouldn't let my father draw the curtains.

'I like to look out at night.'

'There's not one flipping thing to see out there. It's pitch black.'

'I like to see the darkness then.'

I stood by the window and gazed into it and when I heard a car my heart beat wildly but they all passed by.

We had our tea by the fire. I had no appetite, picked at my food and then pushed it aside.

'You must be in a bad way,' said my father, 'if you're off your meat.'

Mrs Clark called in for a while in the evening so I was forced to take my mind off James but even so, he was there hovering in the background, and I was aware of him, like a shadow. And once, when a car did stop outside, I shot out to the door like a rocket fired, only to see a strange man getting out of a strange car.

'How's James?' asked Mrs Clark.

I shrugged.

'You've not quarrelled.'

'A lover's tiff,' said Granny. 'We ken all about them don't we, Mrs Clark?'

Before Mrs Clark left Granny's chin was resting on her chest. Mrs Clark was the best sleeping potion Granny could ever have. Not that she needed much to make her sleep, she had slept well all her life. It was the good clean air, she claimed; her lungs had never been fouled.

Mrs Clark went, I put Granny to bed. Then my father and I settled down in the sitting room for the night. I was sure that I would not sleep but I was dead beat, having been awake most of the previous night, and so in spite of everything (my father snoring, for a start) I fell into a deep sleep full of dreams. Nightmares. James was standing on the ridge high above me and I could not reach him. I was putting up my hand to him calling to him. And then I saw him fall . . . I awoke in a sweat.

It was only seven o'clock but I got up, dressed and went out. The morning was filled with a blue haze, dew lay thick on the grass like scattered sequins. I wanted so much to stay in this place and not go back to the streets of Glasgow and the noisy traffic and the business of plumbing. I stared at the hills, willing James to come from there to here. To me. But he did not.

After breakfast my father said we would leave in an

hour. He wanted to be sure of doing the drive all the way in daylight. He went off into the village to buy a paper.

'Maggie,' said Granny, 'I think you should get your dad to run you to the glen, find James and say you're sorry.'

'But it wasn't my fault.'

'I'm sure he thinks it wasn't his either. One of you's got to lower your pride.'

'Why should it be me?'

'Why should it be him?'

'A girl expects the boy to do it first.'

'Ah, is that right now?' Granny sat back in her chair with her hands clasped on her lap. 'What about all thon stuff you were telling me about the women's freedom thing, or whatever you call it?'

'Liberation.'

'Aye, that. If you believe in all that then you don't have to wait for him do you? Or have I got it wrong?' Sly old thing that she was! She might have been eighty-three going on eighty-four but there was nothing wrong with her head.

I felt cross now. 'Well, anyway, I am not going to him. He was horrible to me first so if he thinks enough of me he'll come to me first. And if he doesn't then I'm not interested!'

My father returned with the paper, I made some coffee. I drank mine slowly. I had not believed that James would not come. I had thought it only a matter of time.

It was time now for us to leave.

'Dinne go away looking such a misery, lass,' said

175

Granny. 'It'll sort itself out. He's a proud lad, you must remember that. You wouldne want one who wasn't, would you?'

I didn't answer that. I didn't know what I wanted right then.

'Will I give him a message if he calls?'

'No! Don't dare, Gran!'

'Come on, Maggie,' said my father, impatient to be away.

I was sorry as usual to leave my granny but my last look was not for her that day. It was for the road that came in from the glen. But there was nothing on it, at least not for me.

CHAPTER FIFTEEN

M**CKINLEY & CAMPBELL,** Plumbing Engineers, were in trouble, deep trouble. It only took me half a day to find that out, in spite of the mess of papers and bills and receipts stuck into the big drawer at the back of the counter. They hadn't been keeping a record of anything, of stock coming in or going out, of bills sent out and monies received or not received, which looked more like it, of bills paid or due.

'Why didn't you just make a note of things as they cropped up?' I asked.

'We didn't have time,' said my father. 'We were run off our feet, your Uncle Tam and I.'

'What about Mum and Aunt Jesse then?'

I might as well have asked what about the moon?

There was, in addition, the income tax return to do. I wasn't sure what expenses exactly we could claim. Everything to do with the shop, I presumed: rent, heat, rates. And then there was V.A.T.!

'Your Aunt Jessie and your mother are allowed a wage out of it,' said my father. 'For acting as receptionists.'

'You haven't been paying them anything,' I objected.

'That's a matter of opinion. After all, part of their

housekeeping could be counted as their wages.'

How much had he and Uncle Tam been taking out of the till every week as wages? They weren't sure. I groaned. You couldn't carry on a business like that. For one thing you'd never know how much profit you were making. One thing I *was* sure of was that we were making a very small profit. Yet Dad claimed that they had been run off their feet, so we should have been doing better.

'Didn't I tell you to write everything down?' I demanded.

They had started off that way, deteriorating swiftly; as soon as I'd turned my back on them.

I stared at the mess spread out along the counter. I didn't know where to begin. I said so.

'We could be doing with one of those accountant fellows,' said Uncle Tam.

'They cost money,' said my father.

Which we didn't have. None of us needed to say that. It was then that I remembered what Mr Fraser had suggested. Could I ring up his father and ask for help. Well, why not?

I did. Grandfather Fraser listened to my long preamble, then said, 'This happens to a lot of people who go into business for the first time. I think I'd better come through and take a look at your accounts.'

'Would you?' It seemed an awful lot to ask.

'Certainly.' He said he'd be delighted.

A big Edinburgh lawyer is coming through to examine our books, I informed the family. James's grandfather. The news threw my mother into a flap and she spent the rest of the day spring-cleaning the shop and flat. I spent it trying to reduce the pieces of paper to some sort of order and realised that there were a number of unpaid bills outstanding, as well as one or two that they had overlooked to send out. My head ached when I went to bed.

Grandfather Fraser arrived early in the morning driving his sleek black car. Sandy went out to look it over. My mother brought down a tray of coffee and fudge cake newly baked by Jean. Everyone appeared in turn to be introduced, Aunt Jessie as well, who kept saying what an honour it was to have James's grandfather here, how fond they were of James, what a fine laddie James was, etc. She would have gone on all day if I hadn't said firmly that we had better get down to business and we didn't want to waste Mr Fraser's time. If she had said James's name one more time I would have had to scream.

'I'll leave you to get on with it then,' she said. 'See you later!' She tripped upstairs to help mother prepare lunch for the guest. They had discussed the menu on the phone for an hour and decided in the end to have frying steak, frozen green beans and mashed potato. I had told them that would do fine, Mr Fraser was not the Duke of Edinburgh, and that they shouldn't make too much fuss.

'Well, Maggie, shall we begin?' He gave me a big smile.

He stayed the whole day with us, working meticulously, writing down figures in his neat hand. It was fascinating to watch him and I learned a lot, he was so systematic.

'You have to be,' he said, 'if you're running a business. It helps in anything.'

No doubt he was right but I thought it unlikely

that I would ever be all that systematic in my life. As a
social anthropologist I would have to be, to a certain
extent, so maybe a big conversion would have to take
place. He did the tax return, showing me how to do it
next time, if there was a next time. He drew up a debit
and credit balance, examined both, came to con-
clusions.

'Are we heading for bankruptcy?' I asked, worried
by his frown.

'Not necessarily. But you'll have to get your father
and uncle to be more efficient. You'll also have to get
them to estimate more keenly for they've obviously not
been getting enough of the bigger jobs that they were
invited to estimate for. All those small jobs might keep
them busy but – ' He spread out his hands.

'Yes.' I felt gloomy at the prospect of encouraging
efficiency in my father who considered that he was an
efficient man already merely because he was not lazy.

'And you'll have to go after your unpaid bills with
more resolution for if you have money standing out it
means you're losing interest.'

Grandfather Fraser gave me a long discourse on
money and business, about half of which I understood.
He then wrote down in simplified fashion all the mea-
sures we had to take.

One: Send out all new bills immediately.

Two: Send out all demands for unpaid bills threatening legal action for those that have been lying more
than three months.

There was a long list to keep us busy. He suggested
also various economies, pinpointed areas where he
thought we might be working uneconomically. But

he thought the most important thing was the working out of the estimates and offered to scrutinise the next one we did before sending it in.

There was, in fact, one lying in the drawer half done. Father had put it there a week ago and forgotten about it.

'That's the very kind of thing that you can't afford to do,' said Mr Fraser, shaking his head sadly. I wondered if he really saw any hope for us in the long run. We were not first-class material, though Sandy, who had been sitting in with us a good part of the time, was showing that he could follow the ins and outs of things quite well. He was good at maths. I decided that he would have to be trained up as our accountant. I asked Mr Fraser if he would speak to my father and uncle when they got back from work. They would never listen to me half so carefully.

They came in, I gave them a cup of tea. Then I said brightly, 'Mr Fraser thinks he sees where we've been going wrong.'

'Oh aye,' said my father.

Mr Fraser cleared his throat, gave them a little general talk on the keeping of accounts etc., to which at least Uncle Tam seemed to be listening enrapt, and then he said that he had been examining their estimates carefully and he thought they were making them too high, which was why they had not been getting the jobs.

'If we made them any lower it wouldn't be worth doing the jobs,' said my father.

'It's better to make a small profit than none.'

'He's right there, Andrew,' said Uncle Tam.

'The thing is to work out your basic costs, of material and labour, and then decide what is the smallest profit you can afford to reasonably make.'

'I dinne like the sound of that,' said my father.

'No, none of us do. But times are hard – I don't need to tell you that, Mr McKinley – and people can't afford high prices. You'll have to try to keep them down.'

Uncle Tam nodded, my father pursed his lips. Mr Fraser proposed that they do this new estimate together. He did most of it, my uncle agreed, and my father did not object. He looked too defeated to make any more objections although Mr Fraser, diplomatically, consulted him on every comma. How to Succeed in Business by Trying. It was quite an education watching Mr Fraser handle my father.

It was nearly seven o'clock by the time Mr Fraser left to drive back to Edinburgh. I hoped he'd be all right. After all, he was seventy, and it had been a long day for him.

'Don't you worry about me, Maggie, I've enjoyed myself, yes I have. And I'll come back, if I may?'

'Of course. Any time.'

All the time, if he wished. With him at the helm we might make a fortune. As it was perhaps now we might just manage to limp through.

'Real nice gent,' said my mother, when we were having tea.

'Quite a big shot isn't he?' said Aunt Jessie, who had been away and come back, not wanting to miss anything.

My father, riled by their admiration for Mr Fraser

(that was as plain as the nose on your face), said, 'I don't know who those so-called big shots think they are coming telling other folks how to run their affairs.'

That riled me. I jumped up and went out for a walk, but not before I told my father one or two things. '*I* asked him to come. He didn't poke his nose in because he'd nothing else to do. He's given us hours of professional advice for nothing and all you can do is gripe.'

'Oh it's not that I'm not grateful, it's just – '

'It's just that you can't bear admitting somebody knows better.'

I had to walk three times round the block to cool off. And whilst I was out, even for those ten minutes, I forgot about plumbing estimates and exasperating parents.

James, why haven't you come? Why haven't you phoned? Why haven't you written?

I had not written or phoned either, naturally not.

We sent in the estimate. We got the job. Everyone was jubilant.

'Our luck's on the turn,' said Uncle Tam.

'I wouldn't count on it,' I said. 'Remember – '

'Oh, aye, we're remembering right enough.'

I bought a second-hand typewriter, began methodically on the list of jobs set down by Mr Fraser. I was determined to be business-like. I told my mother and aunt that they would have to be too.

'Every single thing you do, every sale, you must write down in the book.'

'Every toilet roll?' said Aunt Jessie.

'Yes. You've got to be methodical. Record every

phone call too, both in and out. Keep a note of every enquiry so that we can follow it up.'

'It seems that schooling's done something for her after all,' said my mother.

'Have you been listening?' I was beginning to understand how Mr Scott must feel at times.

'Aye, we've been listening right enough. Haven't we, Jessie?'

'Don't you worry, hen,' said Aunt Jessie. 'When you go back to the school we'll look after things for you.'

'It's not for me! It's for Uncle Tam and Dad. And yourself and Mum.'

They were hopeless! Their attitudes were all wrong. I left them with their knitting and went down town to put a couple of ads in the paper. What had I landed myself with? The running of a plumbing business. Something I had never actually aspired to. McKinley, you're crazy!

In the evenings I studied in the shop with the curtains drawn. The place had become my second home. Every time the phone rang I jumped like a mad frog but it was never him. Sometimes it was a potential customer wanting to make use of the twenty-four-hour service, sometimes it was for Jean or Sandy.

The holidays were coming to a close. I had the books in good order, my father and uncle had work to keep them going for a week or two, and we had prepared yet another estimate.

'You've done well, Maggie,' said my father kind of gruffly. 'I don't know what we'd have done without you.'

Neither did I, and that was some consolation for I realised that I had had no choice. I had had to come home when I did, but I didn't suppose that James would see it like that. His father and mother both earned a regular salary and his grandfather had a lot of money which would one day be theirs. There was never any question of them having to struggle for survival. And I was not sour about that, not at all. It was a matter of luck, and anyway, one day I intended to be in a position where I wouldn't have to struggle either.

Maybe James and I were best apart. Maybe our worlds were too different. Perhaps James had realised that too.

Or perhaps he had decided that, since we had had a break between us, he might as well let it be, for we had often said to one another that we both had years and years of studying ahead of us. Years before we would be established in our careers. And our careers might take us in separate directions.

On the last Saturday before going back to school I went to a party with Isobel. I met her in the street and she said why didn't I come? I could think of no reason not to and I needed a break.

There were lots of friends at the party, some still at school with me, some who had left last summer and were now working. One boy who used to be keen on me attached himself to my side for the evening.

'Where have you been hiding yourself away?' he wanted to know.

'I wish I had the chance to hide!'

I knew where I would go too. I put that thought away as fast as it had come and got up to dance.

The music was loud, the room hot and stuffy. I don't mind loud music, or stuffy rooms either, on occasions, but that happened not to be one of them. Both were killing me. I wanted to escape. I persevered, did my best to enjoy myself. Smile, McKinley! There was nothing wrong with the boy; in fact I used to think he was very much okay. But now he bored me. That was it: more than anything else, I was bored solid.

I took the first opportunity to slip away. Alone, I walked home, preferring it that way than to have the wrong person with me. I shook myself. I would have to snap out of it, I couldn't go on like this.

I wished my granny would write and tell me if she had seen him but she had given up writing letters and when Mrs Clark wrote she said nothing except that Granny was well, Mr Farquharson was asking after me, and so was the nurse. . . .

I was glad to get back to school, to feel the pressure of work building up, to have the exams ahead as a challenge. It cut down the amount of available time for thinking of the unthinkable. For I had decided that that was what James must be, now and forever more.

Even though I was working so hard for my exams I managed to keep an eye on what they were up to in the shop, and Sandy did too. He had started to do the accounts on a Saturday morning and try to make the shop sales balance with what was in the till. My mother and Aunt Jessie had a habit of taking out fifty pence here and a pound there when they needed to run along to the shops for something. I told them, as patiently as I could, that they should write down even that.

'But what difference does it make, Maggie?' asked my mother. 'We'll be getting the money anyway. It's no as if we're taking it from someone else's till.'

'We have to be able to see exactly how much we're making. Or losing.'

After the Highers, Sandy and I were going to stocktake.

'Sounds very grand,' said Aunt Jessie.

'Nothing very grand about it,' I said. 'Counting up washers and stuff!'

If we had to be in business at all I didn't see why it had had to be plumbing. It was just my luck!

My luck did not seem to be all that good these days, certainly not in one compartment of my life. I hoped it would be better when I sat down in front of the examination papers.

'You don't need luck there,' said Mr Scott. 'Just a good bedrock of solid knowledge beneath you. And you've got it, Maggie.'

'Have I?'

I was surprised to be encouraged like this before the event. His usual way was to slam us all unmercifully and tell us how much we were lacking. I said so to Janet.

'Now, that's not true, Maggie,' said Mr Scott. 'I give credit where credit is due.'

'No word at all from James?' asked Janet.

Even to hear his name said aloud bruised me. I shook my head, and she gave me a sympathetic look. Sometimes, when I had a need to speak of him, I went to Janet, for she would listen and understand all that I was saying. She understood my confusion too, for some days I would say I never wanted to see him again and it was all for the best, and on others I would wish and wish that he might come. I did not talk about him at home. My mother said I was young and I'd get over it, which did not mean she was heartless. Aunt Jessie was sorrowful. He'd been a real nice laddie, she'd thought he was daft about me, and she couldn't understand what had gone wrong.

'Not everything lasts, Aunt Jessie,' I said.

But I was still planning to go up to the glen for the summer and had written to the local hotel to ask if they could give me a job as a waitress or chambermaid. I would have to earn money somehow. And James Fraser was not going to keep me away from my glen and my granny. By the time the summer came I hoped I would be strong enough to face him. We might meet on the road, nod or say hello, and then pass on. What an odd idea! And yet I knew that that could happen. It had happened to people before now.

But my heart felt like a ball of lead in my chest.

There were only three days to go until the Highers started, then two. I came downstairs on Saturday morning to open up the shop. It was a lovely May day full of bright sunshine. I regretted that I must spend the day indoors working. I would have liked to walk beneath green trees watching the sunlight filtering through their leaves.

I opened the door and went outside to smell the air. And there, on the pavement, stood James Fraser.

'Hello, Maggie,' he said.

CHAPTER SIXTEEN

'I TRIED not to come. I thought it was for the best. . . .'

'I know, I know.'

I knew how he had felt, what he had thought: he did not have to tell me. We clung to one another in the middle of the pavement. I knew how it must feel to be shipwrecked and then find a piece of dry land.

The window over our heads opened. 'Is that James you have there, Maggie?' called down my mother.

'I hope it's no one else.' I laughed, and squinted up against the morning sun to see her head rimmed in rollers sticking out.

'Bring him up then!'

I did, and a great fuss he had made of him too. My family seemed to have missed him almost as much as I had.

'I kent you would be back,' said my mother, who had known no such thing. She cooked him an enormous breakfast which he did not want but ate out of politeness.

And so I had the day off both from studying and plumbing.

'Away you go, the two of you!' said Aunt Jessie, who became almost delirious with joy when she arrived and saw James. 'We don't need you in the shop, Maggie, and I'm sure you're smart enough to pass all those exams blindfold.'

Whether I was or not was of no importance today. James and I walked beneath green trees and I watched the sunlight filtering through the leaves as I had wished. We talked about the weeks apart, exchanging misery notes. We both apologised for things said.

'I can be horrible,' I said.

'So can I.'

'I can be more horrible.'

He said that he would not allow that, but I knew it to be true for when it comes to dishing out verbal abuse few can surpass me. Walking in the woods with James I resolved to be sweeter, to curtail my tongue. My mother had often said it would get me into real trouble one of these days. I shuddered when I thought how close I had come to never seeing James again.

His family were all fine, he said, when I asked after them. Catriona still had Alexander in tow, his mother was doing a project on insects for her class and the kitchen was full of jars of queer things, some of whom escaped occasionally and crawled about the table, his father was supposed to be making built-in wardrobes for the bedrooms but progress was slow for usually he was to be found lying on one of the beds reading, and Grandfather had gone to stay with a friend in Cannes.

All had been normal in the Fraser household. Except for James.

'I bet your mother's been worried about you?'

'You could say that. She wanted to give me an iron tonic!'

We floated through the day. We made plans for the summer. We would be together in Inverness-shire. We would go to Greenyards together, on a pilgrimage to my great-great-granny's glen. I do not remember exactly where or how we went, but it was predominantly a golden and green day, and at the end of it when James had to catch the last train back to Edinburgh I did not even mind his going for what I'd had had been so very good that it was enough, and I did not know whether I could take any more. I wanted to be alone to think, and gloat.

The first day of the Highers came and went, and I survived. Others followed. Everyone came out of the examination room saying how badly they'd done and they were sure they had failed. There's a funny kind of snobbery that operates against admitting you've done well in an exam or that you like studying. Swot McKinley! I've been called that in my time and can't say it's ever upset me. I was pretty sure I had passed in every subject, and well, though I did not announce it to my fellow candidates. I had no wish to be strung up on the nearest tree. I went and drank coffee with them in a nearby café and talked over the questions and answers. It soon became apparent that many others thought they had passed also. The papers had nearly all been to my liking; I'd felt myself carried away and deeply involved, a feeling I enjoy. Otherwise I wouldn't bother to go to university. I was hoping for at least three A's, perhaps four, or five. There was no harm in hoping, was there?

'None,' said Mr Scott, consenting to smile upon me with favour now that there was no longer any need to bully me. Until next year. I wished that I did not

191

have to do another year at school, that I could go up to university this year instead. But Mr Scott and all my other teachers said that I would benefit from a sixth year and go on to university better equipped. It was all right for them, but I was dying to get moving.

When I had finished my Highers, James sat his A-levels.

I went to Edinburgh the week-end he finished. He thought he had done all right, that he might have scraped through. He was more cautious than I.

'But just think,' I said, 'we are free of all that!'

Free! And the summer lay ahead. A summer to be spent in the north with long light days and short nights when the sky scarcely seems to darken completely.

It was warm that week-end in Edinburgh and there was no wind. For once. Usually you get your head blown off as you come out of Waverley Station. We lay on the grass in Princes Street Gardens. The grass was dotted with people sunbathing and picnicking and listening to the music from the bandstand. It was not my kind of music – brass horns and all that – but out of doors it sounded fine and made you feel you were on holiday. I had felt that way since the exams ended.

We saw Catriona and Alexander going by on one of the paths but they did not see us, not because they were so taken up with one another but because they were both staring at the ground in front of their feet. So many things to look at: trees, flowers (enormous banks of them blazing with colour), the castle, and they were staring at the ground!

When I commented on that to Catriona later, she shrugged. She seemed irritable and said at one point to James and me, 'Oh, why don't you two shut up?' We had been giggling and carrying on in our usual soppy manner. Trying no doubt for onlookers. In bed I asked Catriona, 'Still in love with Alexander?' and she said, 'Of course,' in a rather too lofty voice. Then added dejectedly, 'But we never seem to have much to talk about to one another.'

Hair? What was the matter with hair? Was that not what had brought them together? Couldn't they discuss the latest cuts, which lacquer lasts the longest?

'Oh Maggie, stop it!' She was getting cross so I laid off. I yawned but Catriona wasn't going to allow me to sleep. She confided in me that although she loved Alexander he bored her and she couldn't understand it. 'You and James never seem bored together.' No, that was true, we never were. I smiled at the very idea. We hated going to the pictures together because it cut down on talking time. 'Alexander and I sit in cafés and stare across the table at one another.'

I yawned again. The thought of their boredom bored me, and it seemed obvious to me that Alexander would not last but I did not say so for that was not what Catriona wanted to hear. I told her to let things work through naturally. I'm great at giving advice that I'd never follow myself. Perhaps I could write an advice column for some magazine. *Dear Maggie, Help me . . .* I could hold back sleep no longer. I let myself sink.

Mrs Fraser's attitude towards me was interesting. She appeared to be torn, which I could understand. One half of her was glad that James was no longer miserable, the other regretted the renewal of our friendship. She had another little chat with me when we were shucking peas together in the kitchen.

'I feel you're getting deeper and deeper into this

thing and look at the ages of you! Seventeen and eighteen! Oh I know lots of young people do get married as early as that but not ones who have a long training ahead.'

'Mrs Fraser, we are not thinking of getting married!' How many times did one have to say that before people would believe you? I sneaked a few peas into my mouth. I adore fresh peas and would have eaten the lot if I'd been left on my own. Mrs Fraser did not eat one. Probably thought it was immoral or something. She has some funny ideas. She wouldn't let a loaf of white bread cross the doorstep. Oh, I agree that brown is nicer and better but not all white bread carries rat poison and there's the odd time when I fancy white. James says his mother is a purist. I doubt if anyone will ever use that word to describe me.

Saying goodbye that Sunday evening was not difficult at all for we knew that we would be together again shortly. Our summer up north was about to start.

'See you soon,' said James.

I nodded. I waved all the way up the platform and smiled all the way home on the train.

My family was having a party when I got in. An impromptu affair, which had begun with my father and Uncle Tam going out for a drink and bringing back a carry-out. That meant they had humped back a stout brown paper bag bulging with cans of beer and a bottle of port for the ladies. Aunt Jessie and my mother were quite merry and even my father, who seldom shows it, appeared to be a little under the influence.

'Come away in, hen,' cried my mother. 'Give her a wee drop of port and lemon, Andrew.'

'And how's James?' asked Aunt Jessie fondly.

'Asking after you. All of you.'

'Isn't that nice of him?' Aunt Jessie looked dreamy. 'I went to my fortune-teller last night, Maggie, and do you ken what she told me? There was to be a wedding in the family before the year was out.' Aunt Jessie nodded, sat back with satisfaction. 'What do you make of that then?'

'Nothing. It won't be mine, that's for sure. So unless your Alison's a bit precocious – ' Alison was nine.

My father raised his glass. 'Here's to McKinley and Campbell, the finest plumbing engineers in Glasgow!' We were all prepared to drink to that. 'Aye, things are looking up now.'

'You're a real wee businesswoman, Maggie,' said Aunt Jessie.

'You are that,' agreed Uncle Tam.

My mother and father came in like a chorus. The four of them in turn praised me to the skies, which alerted me at once. They were buttering me up. For what purpose? I waited.

'Maggie, we've been thinking,' said my father, 'and we've decided it would be a good idea to expand the business a bit, try for bigger jobs, maybe even some commercial ones.'

'Why not?' I took a sip of the mixture in my glass. They were all watching me.

'Our old mate Sam Gorman would like to come in with us. He'd bring some money with him.'

'We could do with more capital.'

'And we'd like Sandy to do his apprenticeship with us. We could use him.'

'You're right there.'

'So – ' My father paused before he took the plunge. 'Well, we'd like you to take charge as it were, come in as manageress kind of thing. In fact, we'd need you to organise things for us. You ken what we're like at that side of the business.' He laughed, and Uncle Tam joined in.

'You quite enjoy managing things don't you, Maggie?' butted in Aunt Jessie.

'Yes but – ' I looked at my father. 'How do you mean – come in as manageress?'

'Oh, on a salary like, a good one. I wouldn't expect you to work for nothing.'

'Certainly not,' said Uncle Tam. 'We want to be fair.'

'But I'm going back to school next year.'

'Och Maggie,' said my mother, 'don't you think you could give that up now? You've done your Highers, and you're seventeen after all.'

'But you know I want to go to university.'

'Oh I ken that though I dinne ken what you want to study that anthro–whatever-it-is. You said it was to do with native tribes and their habits – ' She shook her head. She could not go on.

'Aye, what do you want to learn about all that for, Maggie?' asked Aunt Jessie.

'Because it fascinates me,' I cried.

'You'll probably get married before you're twenty,' said my mother. 'Look, why don't you come into the business full-time and help us get going in a bigger way?'

'We need you,' said my father.

'Your dad's right, Maggie,' said Uncle Tam. 'You've a real good head on you for organising things. If you don't come in we couldn't take on Sam Gorman and Sandy. Left to ourselves we'd probably muddle through just making ends meet. We couldn't go into the big time.'

They all murmured assent.

They were fired with the notion of bigger things, and it was I who had first sown the seeds. The responsibility weighed on me like a ton load of bricks.

'You don't have to give us your answer straight away,' said my father. He was already beginning to act a bit more like the head of the firm. Crazy! 'You can think it over and let us know.'

I nodded. I felt stunned. They sat in a semi-circle smiling at me. In their minds the empire was forming, I was sitting at a big polished desk answering a battery of telephones.

I got up. 'Think I'll go for a walk.'

'It's dark out,' said my mother.

'I don't mind the dark.' I told her to relax, I would not go far and I would stay in well-lit places.

I was glad to get out of the room and breathe again. They wanted me to give up everything and come into the plumbing business. It was monstrous, monstrous! I wanted to go to university. And I wanted not only to study the customs of primitive peoples but to go to Central Australia, Peru, Borneo, New Guinea, Mexico, Africa, any of them, all of them, the first chance I got. I did not want to stay in Glasgow taking in orders for plumbing and waiting for some man to come and release me by slipping a diamond ring over the fourth finger of my left hand. I raged at the moon which hung limpidly above the rooftops. But after a bit I subsided, and my anger turned to dejection. They were not being selfish, no more than anyone else, and from their point of view it all made sense. They had never taken the idea of my career seriously, to them it made as much sense as going to the moon, and now that I had James they thought I should see it in the same way. I could probably make the business go and they couldn't. I could make the difference for my family and Uncle Tam's between just scraping along and having money to live pretty well. Was I exaggerating? I hoped so. But even if I was I knew I could help them, and they needed help. Could I turn my back on them. Could I afford not to?

It was a terrible situation to be caught in. I walked for miles through the quiet streets talking it out in my head, considering it this way and that, and tormenting myself whatever way I considered it. There was no satisfactory answer. But I had to take a decision. And in fact, I had already taken one, long before I stopped arguing with myself. I had known all along that there was only one thing I could do, or must do.

My father was still up when I came home, my mother had gone to bed, and my aunt and uncle had left. He was drinking a cup of tea. He had been waiting for me.

'Have you thought?'

I nodded. I sat down beside him. 'Dad, I – ' I shook my head.

'You can't do it? I had a feeling you wouldn't. The others thought you would but somehow I knew.'

'I'm sorry. But, you see, I need to make my own life. *I must.*'

'I understand, lassie. But there was no harm in hoping.' He sighed. 'It was a bit of a wild fancy maybe, us all in big business. And I canne really stop you going. I did it myself. My father didn't want me to leave the glen, he'd have liked it fine if I'd joined the Forestry.'

I poured him another cup of tea, took one myself. We drank together. I would still help out whenever I could, I promised, and I said that I thought he should take Sandy as an apprentice for Sandy showed signs of being good at the business side and might eventually be able to manage it.

'I'll do my best to train him.'

'Okay, lass. And don't think too ill of us for asking you.'

'I won't. Don't think too ill of me for refusing.'

'We won't.'

My mother would not take it as well but he would talk to her and I could not help it even if she did feel I had let her down. I don't know how it's possible to live without letting people down sometimes. When I lay in bed afterwards I thought about that. For there would be another problem ahead, not so large but still important. They would ask me to give up my summer up north and stay at home to help with the business. They would think I ought to since they were going to keep me at school for one more year. Part of me felt I ought to as well. But I had promised James and my granny and they were important too. Very important. And I had had to let them down at Easter. I tossed and turned.

In the morning I was exhausted and limp, but felt strangely peaceful for I had taken two vital decisions, and it had come to me, in the midst of taking them, that the only thing one can do is to try to make up one's mind what to do for the best and then hold to it. It was not only crazy to try to please everybody, it was not possible.

I had decided to go north for the two months of summer. I would stay with my granny, work at the hotel and earn some money which I would save for the coming year, and then I would go with James up to Strathcarron in Easter Ross and find Greenyards.

And I had decided what my first choice of university was going to be. It would be Edinburgh.